"We'll have the tests done soon."

Sam glared at Marcie as he prepared to leave. "And in the meantime, I don't want you anywhere near my daughter."

Marcie nodded. She understood Sam's anger for what it was...fear of losing the child he loved.

She studied his broad back as he walked away. His stride was still determined if not quite as confident as when he'd arrived. She could imagine him teaching her daughter—his daughter—*Kyla* to play softball, fighting anyone who tried to harm her, comforting her after a bad dream...yet he was helpless now. She could imagine his frustration and dread.

As if he felt her gaze, Sam turned.

Across the room, against all logic, she felt a bond flow between them. Irrationally she wanted to go to him, take him into her arms and comfort him, let him

For the

Dear Reader,

Silhouette Romance is celebrating the month of valentines with six very special love stories—and three brand-new miniseries you don't want to miss. *On Baby Patrol,* our BUNDLE OF JOY selection, by bestselling author Sharon De Vita, is book one of her wonderful series, LULLABIES AND LOVE, about a legendary cradle that brings love to three brothers who are officers of the law.

In *Granted: Big Sky Groom,* Carol Grace begins her sparkling new series, BEST-KEPT WISHES, in which three high school friends' prom-night wishes are finally about to be granted. Author Julianna Morris tells the delightful story of a handsome doctor whose life is turned topsy-turvy when he becomes the guardian of his orphaned niece in *Dr. Dad.* And in Cathleen Galitz's spirited tale, *100% Pure Cowboy,* a woman returns home from a mother-daughter bonding trip with the husband of her dreams.

Next is *Corporate Groom,* which starts Linda Varner's terrific new miniseries, THREE WEDDINGS AND A FAMILY, about long-lost relatives who find a family. And finally, in *With This Child...,* Sally Carleen tells the compelling story of a woman whose baby was switched at birth—and the single father who will do anything to keep his child.

I hope you enjoy all six of Silhouette Romance's love stories this month. And next month, in March, be sure to look for *The Princess Bride* by bestselling author Diana Palmer, which launches Silhouette Romance's new monthly promotional miniseries, VIRGIN BRIDES.

Regards,

Joan Marlow Golan
Senior Editor

Please address questions and book requests to:
Silhouette Reader Service
U.S.: 3010 Walden Ave., P.O. Box 1325, Buffalo, NY 14269
Canadian: P.O. Box 609, Fort Erie, Ont. L2A 5X3

WITH THIS CHILD...

Sally Carleen

Silhouette

R O M A N C E™

Published by Silhouette Books

America's Publisher of Contemporary Romance

To MHS Class of '63

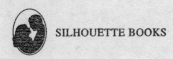

SILHOUETTE BOOKS

ISBN 0-373-19281-9

WITH THIS CHILD...

Copyright © 1998 by Sally B. Steward

Printed in U.S.A.

Books by Sally Carleen

Silhouette Romance

An Improbable Wife #1101
Cody's Christmas Wish #1124
My Favorite Husband #1183
Porcupine Ranch #1221
With This Child... #1281

Silhouette Shadows

Shaded Leaves of Destiny #46

SALLY CARLEEN

For as long as she can remember, Sally planned to be a writer when she grew up. Finally one day, after more years than she cares to admit, she realized she was as grown-up as she was likely to become, and began to write romance novels. In the years prior to her epiphany, Sally supported her writing habit by working as a legal secretary, a real-estate agent, a legal assistant, a leasing agent, an executive secretary and in various other occupations.

She now writes full time and looks upon her previous careers as research and/or torture. A native of McAlester, Oklahoma, and naturalized citizen of Dallas, Texas, Sally now lives in Lee's Summit, Missouri, with her husband, Max, their very large cat, Leo, and a very small dog, Cricket. Her interests, besides writing, are chocolate and Coca-Cola Classic.

Readers can write to Sally at P.O. Box 6614, Lee's Summit, MO 64086.

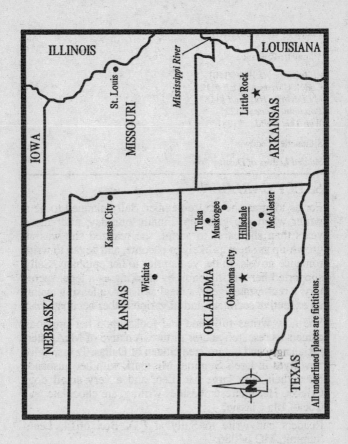

ILLINOIS

LOUISIANA

St. Louis •

Mississippi River

Little Rock ★

MISSOURI

ARKANSAS

IOWA

Kansas City •

Tulsa •
Muskogee •

McAlester •

Hillsdale •

NEBRASKA

Wichita •

KANSAS

OKLAHOMA

Oklahoma City ★

N

TEXAS

All underlined places are fictitious.

Prologue

I switched your baby for theirs. You buried their child. Your baby is alive.

Cars zipped past on the street in front of Marcie Turner. A locust chirruped from a nearby tree. A dog barked in the distance. The world around her continued, while Marcie stood frozen in the heat of Tulsa in July, staring uncomprehendingly at the last two lines of the letter.

A neighbor approached the mailboxes where Marcie stood, and she knew she had to move. She had to get inside, before anyone else came by, before anyone else saw her so completely out of control.

Moving like a robot, she unlocked the security door, entered the air-conditioned lobby of the building and took the elevator to the fifth floor, to the security and privacy of her condo.

She went inside, closed the door behind her, turned the dead bolt and put on the chain, as if she could lock out the sorrow and fear that lurked just over her shoulder, the way she'd locked them out for years.

Her footsteps made no sound as she crossed the plushly carpeted living room, and for one crazy moment, she wondered if this was all a dream, if she even existed at all.

She slid onto a stool at the polished walnut breakfast bar and studied the envelope again, the ominous message that had prompted her to rip open the letter the moment she pulled it from the mailbox.

To be delivered to Marcie Turner at my death.

It had Dr. Franklin's return address, and Marcie had known immediately that it could only relate to one thing.

Her hands trembled as she forced herself to read the two typewritten pages again, to see if she'd imagined the insane story they had to tell:

Dear Marcie:
I must be dead or you wouldn't be reading this.

I can't go to meet my Maker with this secret on my soul, but I don't have the guts to tell you face-to-face.

You know I've always wanted the best for you, and so has your mama.

It wasn't easy on her raising you alone after your daddy died when you were just a little thing. It hit her hard when you got pregnant your junior year in high school. Raising that baby would have made it tough for you to get a good education and have a better life than she did.

You were always so easy-going, and your mama thought at first she could talk you into giving your baby up for adoption, but I knew you'd never agree to that. When I gave you the news, your whole face lit up with love, and I knew this would be the first time you defied your mama.

I guess you think I'm taking my time getting to the

point, but to tell the truth, I'm not all that anxious to get there. My head thinks I did the right thing, but my heart's not so sure.

To get on with it, right after you had your baby, I did an emergency C-section on another woman. Did you know Lisa Kramer? She was a few years older than you, and her folks lived a little ways outside of town, so you might not have. Anyway, she was a real nice girl. Married a fellow named Sam Woodward that she met at college, and they moved to McAlester so he could coach football at the high school. But she came back home to have her baby. That baby had a defective heart, only lived a few hours. Lisa had problems, and I had to do a hysterectomy.

Your baby, however, was born alive and kicking. Your mama was there, of course, and while you were resting and Lisa was in the recovery room, we went down to the cafeteria to get a cup of coffee. I was pretty upset, knowing Lisa's baby was dying and I couldn't do a damn thing about it. I'd already told Sam, and he was all broken up. I dreaded telling Lisa when she came out of the anaesthetic. I knew how much she wanted children, what a good mother she would have been, what a nice fellow Sam seemed like.

Your mama said it was a shame Lisa's baby wouldn't live when it would have had such a good life, and it was a shame your baby, precious as she was, would ruin your life and have a tough time growing up with a single mother. She sat there in the hospital cafeteria and looked at me, and I knew what she was thinking even before she said it.

Marcie, I want you to know this wasn't an easy decision for either of us. We both wanted to do what was best for you and for your baby. I falsified all the

records, and only your mama, my nurse and I know
the truth. Lisa and Sam never knew their baby died.

May God forgive me because you probably never
will, I switched your baby for theirs.

You buried their child. Your daughter is alive.

Marcie lowered the pages to the wooden surface of the
bar. She needed a drink...iced tea, wine, a soft drink, water,
anything wet. But she couldn't seem to move.

It wasn't possible. She'd have known if her baby was
alive.

She'd dreamed about her every night that first year, but
surely that was normal, didn't mean anything.

After she managed to lock away the pain, the dreams
had stopped.

Now this letter, almost thirteen years later, was asking
her to unlock that pain, to think about her baby again, to
hope and pray and dream that she was alive, that she'd be
able to see her and hold her.

She couldn't do that.

Dr. Franklin had been old, probably senile. She'd pitch
this insane letter and get on with the life she'd so pains-
takingly built for herself.

But she couldn't do that, either. It was too late.

Even this glimmer of hope had revived the old pain, the
old love.

If there was even the slightest chance her child was alive,
she had to know.

Chapter One

Marcie drove slowly down the small neighborhood streets of McAlester, Oklahoma. As she stared out the window, carefully following the directions given her by the detective she'd hired to find her daughter, her fingers fidgeted with the envelope containing everything she had of her baby— the letter from Dr. Franklin, the detective's report, and pictures of Kyla and Sam Woodward.

Kyla Woodward...twelve years old...thirteen next month... Going into eighth grade...active in sports... Lisa Woodward died seven years ago...congenital heart problems... Sam Woodward, coach of high school football team...coaches Kyla's softball team... Neighbors say they're a happy, well-adjusted family.

She'd read the report until she knew it by heart, looked at those photographs a thousand times, memorizing every detail, searching for her features in Kyla Woodward's face.

Her mother, embarrassed at being caught but unrepentant, had verified Dr. Franklin's story, but still Marcie had held back. She couldn't face the possibility of holding her daughter, only to have that child yanked away because her mother and Dr. Franklin were wrong.

Over the past couple of days, she'd swung wildly from guarded certainty one minute to doubt and confusion the next.

She had no idea what to do now.

She had no idea why she was searching for their house.

What would she do if she saw Kyla? What would she say to her? To Sam?

She turned onto Maple Street, one hand clutching the envelope in her lap. According to the directions, Sam Woodward's house was at the end of the third block down. Even though she couldn't see it from this distance, she could feel its presence.

Claustrophobia suddenly overwhelmed her, making her feel trapped in her small car, propelled by forces beyond her control into a scary unknown world. She wasn't ready for this, to know for sure whether her baby was alive, to risk seeing her only to lose her again.

Marcie lowered the windows, breathing deeply, focusing on everything around her except that house three blocks away.

It was an older, established neighborhood. Huge trees formed a canopy over the street and colorful flowers bloomed everywhere.

Scents she'd almost forgotten assailed her—freshly cut grass, honeysuckle, roses, and all the other fragrances that never reached her fifth-floor condo in Tulsa.

A small boy in a blue sunsuit pedaled his tricycle across the street in front of her.

A young couple diligently painted a house they appeared to be restoring.

An elderly woman puttered in her flower beds.

A tiny Yorkie darted to the end of a sidewalk to bark frantically as Marcie drove past.

Saturday morning in a small town.

Several cars were parked in the street—a common problem with houses too old to have garages—but other than that, the area seemed well cared-for. The detective had told her that much; had assured her that while Sam Woodward might not be getting rich working as a high school football coach, he appeared to be providing well for his daughter. Her daughter.

There was absolutely nothing in this well-kept, comfortable neighborhood to send nervous chills down Marcie's spine, to cause her palms to sweat, her hands to tremble as they clutched the steering wheel.

Nothing except the two-story white house that seemed to be approaching her, rather than vice versa.

Seeing the picture of the house hadn't prepared her for the sense of isolation the actual structure made her feel, the sense of total separation from everything inside it.

From Sam and Kyla Woodward.

She drove past, her gaze skimming over the detached garage to scan the front porch, the open windows and doors, searching for a glimpse of the blond girl in the pictures.

She turned the corner to go around the side of the house—

And a baseball slammed onto the hood of her car, followed by a young girl and then a dull thud. Marcie swerved to the side of the road, crushing the brake to the floor, while adrenaline exploded through her body.

Oh, God! She'd just run down her daughter!

Her breath caught in her chest as she shifted into park. The trees and houses and everything else around her blurred as that moment in time locked on itself, filling her vision with the sight of the girl slamming against her car.

"I'm sorry, lady!"

Marcie jumped at the sound of the words coming from the passenger window.

The beautiful child from the pictures, now distressed instead of laughing, peered at her from wide blue eyes.

From the same blue eyes Marcie saw in the mirror every morning.

In that instant, she knew, and in spite of the black fear that hovered around the edges of her soul, happiness burst over Marcie like sunrise after a night filled with terrors.

Her baby wasn't dead. She was alive, breathing, speaking.

A thousand words and a thousand emotions lumped in Marcie's throat, and she had to blink back sudden tears as she gazed at her child in the flesh only a few feet away. She wanted to fly across the distance, grab her and hold her in her arms, tightly enough to make up for all the years she hadn't been able to hold her. She wanted to laugh, to cry, to live the thirteen years separating them in one burst...to reclaim her baby.

Instead, she sat behind the wheel of her car, paralyzed, unable even to speak.

And the child she'd carried inside her body, given birth to, shared the same hair and eyes with, that child looked at her as if she were a stranger.

Which she was.

Cold darkness pressed against her, throwing a shadow over her joy.

"Don't cry, ma'am. We'll pay to have your car fixed." The girl inclined her head toward the hood. "It didn't make much of a dent, anyway. You hardly notice it." She smiled tentatively. "And I didn't even make a dent at all when I ran into you."

A tall, muscular man wearing cut-offs and a T-shirt jogged over from the yard and put an arm possessively about her daughter's shoulders.

Sam Woodward.

The man who'd raised her baby and given her the laughter she'd seen in the photographs her detective took.

The man she was grateful to and resentful of. The man she envied and feared beyond all reason.

He leaned over and peered in the window, his face beside her daughter's. "Are you all right?"

She forced herself to nod, though she was as far from *all right* as it was possible to be.

He went around to the hood of the car, peered closely at a spot and traced a small circle with one finger of a large hand, a hand big enough to catch footballs.

She didn't want to look at him. She wanted to focus on her daughter, to never let her out of her sight again, to never risk losing her again.

But her gaze involuntarily followed him, her mind racing, as she tried to think of what she should say.

With a scowl, he walked around to the driver's side window. He had a kind face, tanned, with laugh lines like sunbursts accenting his clear hazel eyes. Unruly brown hair tumbled over his forehead, imbuing him with a rakish innocence.

"My daughter's right," he said. "The ball didn't leave a very big dent at all. I have a friend who works on cars. He can probably pop it out for you today without even hurting the paint."

My daughter?

No! she wanted to scream. *She's my daughter! You can't have her!*

She lifted a shaky hand to her forehead.

"Of course, you can take your car wherever you want and get it fixed, and I'll pay for it," Sam continued, apparently mistaking the reason for her confusion.

She had to say something, she had to tell them.

"Why don't you get out and come sit on the porch for

a few minutes?'' Sam asked in a concerned voice. "You seem kind of shaken up. Kyla—that's my daughter—she'll fix you a glass of iced tea and you can catch your breath.''

Kyla.

Not *Jenny,* but *Kyla.*

She hadn't even been able to choose her daughter's name. She'd given her baby's name to Sam and Lisa Woodward's baby. She'd buried their child with her daughter's name.

Sam opened her car door and extended his hand to help her, as if she were an invalid.

It was an accurate assumption. Her brain and body had shut down, ceased to function. She had no idea what to say, and wasn't sure she'd be able to speak if she did know.

She shut off the engine and accepted Sam's hand. It was big and competent and gave her a protected feeling. As she slid from the car and stood, he placed his other hand at the small of her back, steadying her, as if she were fragile and likely to stumble.

She squelched a nervous giggle at the irony. Sam Woodward was helping her, making her feel protected and secure. Sam Woodward, whose life she'd come to destroy.

Kyla bounced up beside her as they came around the car. "Dad was teaching me to catch pop flies, and that one got away. I'm really sorry.''

"It's okay," Marcie said, the words coming out barely above a whisper. "I thought I hit *you.* I thought you were hurt.''

"Nah. I ran into your car 'cause I wasn't watching where I was going. Hardly anybody ever comes down that street, but Dad's always yelling at me for running out.'' She grinned at Sam. "Guess he's right once in a while. I'll go fix you some tea. You want sugar and lemon?''

"Yes.'' She smiled. "Yes, please. I'd like that.'' She

didn't usually take sugar and lemon, but she'd have taken salt if her daughter offered it.

Her baby was there, in person, real, alive.

Kyla sprinted up the walk and into the house ahead of them, a happy, secure, obviously loved child, with no clue that she'd just met her mother.

They reached the porch, and Sam indicated a scattering of wrought-iron chairs with faded green-and-white striped cushions. Marcie sank into the closest one, grateful that she was no longer dependent on her shaky legs to hold her up.

"I'm Sam Woodward." He offered his hand again, and she clasped it for the second time. His shake was firm and confident, and she was amazed at how much she liked him, in spite of everything.

He was the personification of a high school football coach. His open, friendly smile—the same smile she'd seen in his pictures, but even more potent in person—promised carefree autumn evenings at football games and wiener roasts in the park.

Sam looked at her oddly, and Marcie realized she hadn't told him who she was. She smiled nervously. "I'm Marcie Turner. I, uh—" *I'm Kyla's mother?* No, that probably wasn't a good way to establish her identity.

Sam took the chair beside her, looking at her expectantly, waiting for her to finish her sentence. She couldn't think of anything to say except *I'm Kyla's mother.* Every crevice in her mind was filled with that thought, leaving no room for coherency.

"I'm an accountant," she finally blurted, then wondered why she'd said it. An attempt to offer some sort of validation that she existed, that she had an identity and a life, that she wasn't really as disconnected as she felt right now?

"That must come in handy around April fifteenth," Sam replied, as if their conversation were perfectly normal. And maybe it was. Right now, she had no idea of what was and wasn't normal. "I'm the high school football coach," he continued.

"I know."

"Then you're from McAlester,"

"No. I live in Tulsa. I just meant you look like a football coach. All those muscles." Oh, God! What on earth was she saying? "I don't make a habit of running into...people."

"Relax. You didn't. Kyla ran into you. First I bounced a softball off the hood of your car, then my kid plowed into you."

"Teenager," Kyla corrected, pushing open the screen door with her hip and emerging carrying three large glasses of tea on a tray. "I'm almost a teenager, and Dad's having a hard time accepting that I'm practically grown up."

Your mother's having a hard time accepting that, too! Marcie wanted to shout.

"That's because you're not practically grown up, missy," Sam replied. "Not even close."

Marcie accepted a tall drink from Kyla, trying not to stare at her, to let her eyes feast only in short, hungry glances. Her teeth chattered against the rim of the glass, but she managed to swallow several large gulps of the cold liquid.

Kyla sprawled in another chair. "Pretty soon I'll be dating, and next thing you know, you'll be a grandfather."

Marcie choked on her tea, and Sam leaned over to pat her on the back.

"You okay?" he asked solicitously when she caught her breath.

Marcie nodded and forced a smile. "That was, um, kind of shocking. I mean, I know you were teasing. It's just that you're so young, and..." Her voice trailed off, and she took another drink of her tea to cover her confusion.

Sam chuckled. "My impertinent daughter is baiting me. It's one of her favorite pastimes."

Kyla grinned mischievously. "Keeps him on his toes. It's a tough job, but somebody's gotta do it, and I'm an only child. Are you married? Do you have any kids?"

Marcie froze at the last question, but Sam saved her from having to figure out how to answer it.

"Kyla!" he exclaimed, but he smiled as he looked at Marcie. "My kid may be totally tactless, but she has no manners."

"Oh, Dad," Kyla groaned. "It's a good thing you can coach football, 'cause you'd sure never make it as a co-median."

He leaned over and yanked on her blond ponytail, and burning, icy envy washed over Marcie.

Being with her daughter was making her feel impossibly distant from her. Kyla and Sam shared a closeness she wanted desperately, but wasn't sure she could ever have.

Her daughter was happy and loved, that was obvious. Perhaps she should leave it at that, get up, set down her glass of tea, thank the two of them politely and walk away, out of Kyla's life. Marcie had dealt with the pain of losing her once, and that pain had been diffused and pointless. Now, if she knew it was for Kyla's benefit, surely she could do it again. Perhaps that would be the kindest, most loving thing she could do for her daughter.

No.

Her own mother had done what she thought best for Marcie, and it hadn't been the best at all. Marcie should have had the right to make her own decisions.

Now she *would* give her daughter that right. If Kyla should decide she wanted nothing to do with her real mother, then Marcie would have to somehow force herself to walk out of her life, to again learn to live with emptiness.

Whatever the outcome, the decision belonged to Kyla.

Marcie suddenly realized Sam and Kyla were staring at her curiously.

She rose on shaky legs, setting her tea on the small wrought-iron table.

"I, uh..." No, she couldn't just blurt it out like that. "I'd better be going. Thank you for the tea."

"You sure you're okay to drive?" Sam asked.

She tried a confident smile, but knew it came out weak and uncertain. "I'm sure."

She moved numbly down the cracked sidewalk, with Sam on one side and Kyla on the other. At the end of the walk, her silver compact car reflected the sunlight in a painful glare as it lured and repelled at the same time—offering escape from this unknown, frightening situation, while taking her away from her daughter.

Sam opened her car door for her, as if speeding her exit, getting her out of his life, away from the child she'd given birth to but he claimed as his daughter.

"If you have a pencil, I'll write down my name and address so you can call me about that dent," he said.

"I don't need your address. I—" She stopped herself before she could blurt out why she didn't need his name and address, that she already knew it. She knew his age and where he worked and how long he'd been there and his social security number and when his wife had died...and the name of the hospital where Kyla had been born.

But this wasn't the right time to tell him that. She had to carry through with the charade. She retrieved her purse from the floorboard and, hands shaking noticeably, withdrew a pen and a small notepad, then offered it to him.

He scribbled something and returned it to her. Without looking, she shoved it into her purse.

"Thank you," she said.

He closed the door, stepped back from the car, wrapped

one arm around Kyla and smiled his wonderful, carefree smile again. She found her own lips turning up in answer, as if something deep inside couldn't resist being sucked into such complete happiness.

Kyla lifted a hand to wave. "Bye, Marcie! Sorry 'bout your car."

"Goodbye...Kyla." Time seemed to freeze as Marcie gazed at Kyla, unable to break the last contact with her, but unable to do anything about it. She wasn't sure whether she'd been staring for a second or an hour.

"So long, Ms. Turner," Sam said, breaking the spell.

With a quick wave, Marcie started the engine and drove down the block. Her heart threatened to pound its way out of her chest, her mouth was dry, and her thoughts darted past in unrecognizable, kaleidoscopic images.

She headed for the highway, for the fastest way home. Once inside her condo, she could lock the doors and draw the blinds and feel safe.

Except she feared she'd never be safe there again. Always she'd be trying to find a way to reach her daughter—and terrified of what would happen when she succeeded.

As Marcie Turner drove away, Sam tugged on Kyla's ponytail again. "What happened to your manners? Wash them down the drain when you showered this morning?"

"You told me you never learn anything if you don't ask questions."

"There are questions and there are questions, and asking a strange woman if she's married and has children pretty much pushes the limits."

Kyla shrugged and gazed toward the corner where Marcie's car had just disappeared from view. "Yeah," she said thoughtfully, "she did get a funny look when I asked her that."

That she had, Sam thought. In fact, Marcie Turner had been a whole review of *funny looks*.

"Well, I was just checking her out for your benefit. She's a real babe."

Sam groaned. "Go get your softball." He pointed down the street.

With Kyla's own burgeoning awareness of the opposite sex, she'd begun to tease him unmercifully about women. And this time she'd nailed him.

In spite of Marcie's nervousness, he'd found himself attracted to her. Even in khaki shorts and a plain white blouse, she had an air about her. Her shiny golden hair fell straight to her shoulders, catching and reflecting the sunlight. In the sweltering heat of the July afternoon, she'd seemed cool and aloof, yet strangely vulnerable.

She looked familiar, in an eerie sort of way. Something about her had tickled around the edges of his memory, nagging him with a resemblance he couldn't quite place. He was positive that he didn't know her, but just as positive that he should.

"And how about when you called her by her first name?" he shouted after Kyla.

Kyla stopped, turned back to look at him and tilted her head to one side. Her face, soft with the remnants of childhood yet edged with the approach of maturity, mirrored his confusion about the woman. "I didn't think about it. It was like I'd known her a real long time or something." She shrugged, grinned and trotted the rest of the way to retrieve her ball.

So Kyla had noticed the odd familiarity about the woman, too.

Well, they'd probably seen her somewhere, at the grocery store or one of Kyla's softball games or the school's football games.

Except she lived in Tulsa.

Heck, she probably resembled some television star. She was a *babe,* that was for sure.

Sam shoved his hands into the pockets of his cutoffs and turned to walk back to the house.

Directly in front of him, where it must have fallen from Marcie Turner's car, was a large manila envelope.

He picked it up, hoping it contained an address, so that he could return it. She hadn't seemed too likely to contact him again.

Not that he was looking for an excuse to contact her, no matter how much of a *babe* she was. Okay, maybe he had taken her hand and put his arm around her waist to help her out of the car when it probably wasn't necessary. And he'd certainly enjoyed the contact.

He smiled at himself and his daughter and life in general as he opened the envelope...

...and found a letter-size envelope inside, along with several typewritten pages and pictures of his house, himself and Kyla.

A cold hand wrapped around and squeezed his heart.

What the hell was going on? Why did this woman have pictures of his home and his daughter? Was she stalking them? Was that why she'd seemed familiar? Had he seen her in crowds, watching them?

Her assertion that she didn't need his address replayed itself in his head.

No wonder she hadn't needed it.

She already had it.

"What's that, Pops?"

Sam fumbled the pictures and letter back into the envelope. "Nothing." He wasn't going to have Kyla frightened.

"Looks like something to me." Tossing the ball into the air and catching it, she walked beside him as he strode back to the house.

"Papers. Marcie Turner's papers."

"Kyla!" The familiar shout came from across the street.
"Wanna ride bikes for a while?"

"Sure, Rachel! Be right there." She handed Sam the
ball. "You don't mind, do you, Dad? Rachel's having a
tough time since her mom and dad split up."

He looked into his daughter's beautiful, concerned face.
Maybe because she had no mother, she'd taken on the role
of caring for any of her friends who had problems. Or
maybe she did it just because she was a wonderful, caring
kid, his own personal angel.

"Of course I don't mind. I'll be glad to get a little rest
from playing ball with you!" He grinned, trying to main-
tain their usual banter, hoping his grin wasn't as shaky as
it felt.

She ran toward the garage to get her bike, long legs
flying in the gracefully awkward manner of fawns and
twelve-year-olds, and he loved her so much it hurt.

They'd almost lost her the night she was born. He still
remembered the agony when Dr. Franklin had told him she
had a fatal heart defect and wouldn't live through the night.

And he still remembered the incredible joy when she had
survived the night, in defiance of the doctor's death sentence.

Knowing they could have no more children, he and Lisa
had spoiled Kyla shamelessly from that day forward. In
fact, Lisa had devoted herself totally to Kyla, even to the
extent of ignoring him. But he'd accepted that. He'd understood how much she hurt when the doctor told her about
the hysterectomy, how frightened she was each day that the
doctor's prophecy about Kyla's death would come true.

Kyla had been Lisa's priority, and five years later, as she
lay dying from the same heart disease the doctor had di-
agnosed in Kyla, she'd made Sam promise to take care of
their child.

Not that such a promise was necessary. He'd gladly lay down his life for his daughter.

Whatever Marcie Turner was up to, he'd stop her. Whatever it took, he'd protect his daughter.

He carried the envelope inside, sat down at the kitchen table and dumped out the contents. The smaller envelope was a letter addressed to Marcie in Tulsa. So at least he had the woman's address, he thought grimly. And he *would* take this to the police.

But then he noticed the return address—Elton Franklin, the doctor who'd delivered Kyla. Suffocating heat flushed his body, prickling his skin, making breathing difficult.

He'd worried about Kyla for the past twelve—almost thirteen—years, terrified every time she caught cold or had a childhood disease. And he'd berated himself for that worrying, telling himself it didn't accomplish a blasted thing, but unable to stop doing it.

Now…today…into his life came Marcie Turner with her pictures of the two of them and a letter addressed to her from Lisa's doctor. Were all his concerns being validated? Did this letter contain a death sentence for Kyla?

But if it did, why was it addressed to Marcie Turner?

He had to open that letter and read it.

Sam stared at the envelope for several minutes. He regularly bench-pressed two-hundred-pound weights, but he couldn't seem to find the strength to lift that little bit of paper weighing less than an ounce.

He wiped his sweaty palms on his cutoffs, then drew a shaky hand across his mouth and chin. His face was damp with perspiration.

Moving rapidly, so that he wouldn't have a chance to chicken out, he yanked the letter from inside the envelope and unfolded the two pages.

Chapter Two

Marcie clutched the steering wheel with damp, sticky hands and made herself focus on the task of driving, on actions that normally came automatically. But not today. Today, leaving Sam's house, she had to concentrate, to remind herself which pedal to use, to stop at red lights, go on green, turn the wheel at corners.

Her brain, her heart, her entire body, screamed in protest at the overload of emotions. She'd found her daughter alive, talked to her, met the man who'd inadvertently stolen her daughter. And then she'd had to walk quietly away.

Reaching the highway that led to the turnpike, she pulled into a convenience store and parked at the side. Out of the main traffic area, she finally let loose, laid her head in her hands and allowed earthquake tremors to shake her body, while tears spilled between her fingers.

In a minute she'd pull herself together, go into the store and get a cola, then get home as fast as she could. Once in her safe haven, she'd think about everything, about Kyla and what she ought to do next. Right now, she couldn't face it, couldn't deal with the huge explosions of happiness and anger and disbelief and sheer terror.

Finally, the tremors subsided, as some of the unbearable tension dissipated. She snatched a handful of tissues from the box in the back seat and dried her eyes.

This wasn't like her, she thought, to completely lose control. But these were not usual circumstances.

She pushed her hair back from her face. She had to get home and figure out what to do next.

Needing to reassure herself that everything that had just happened was real, she looked around for the envelope containing her pictures of Kyla, along with the detective's report and the letter from Dr. Franklin.

It wasn't in her lap.

Or on the passenger seat beside her.

She slid out of the car and searched under the seats, in the back...everywhere. Her movements became more frantic with each empty space she encountered. Her hands trembled as she searched for the second time.

She stepped back from the car and looked at it in disbelieving horror.

The envelope was gone.

It could only have fallen from her lap when she got out at Sam's house.

Either her pictures were lying in the street, being run over by cars, or Sam and Kyla had noticed them and picked them up.

In that quiet neighborhood, the latter seemed more likely.

By now, Sam and Kyla probably knew the truth.

This wasn't the way she'd wanted her daughter to find out.

Her mind whirling with black despair and chaos, she sank into the car and closed the door behind her.

With one stupid act, she'd made a terrible situation worse. She needed to get home as fast as possible.

But her fingers refused to turn the key.

She had to face the consequences of her actions. She couldn't blame her mother or Dr. Franklin for this latest disaster.

In fact, maybe she had to take some of the blame for everything. Would things be different if she'd paid more attention when her baby was born, if she'd asked more questions about the death?

She'd been in shock, stunned by the loss, overwhelmed by guilt, convinced that the death was somehow her fault, because she'd been so stubborn, because she'd refused to consider her mother's plan of adoption. So she'd allowed Dr. Franklin and her mother to take charge.

She'd asked to hold her child once before they took her away forever, to bury her in the cold, impersonal earth, but Dr. Franklin and her mother had persuaded her not to. She'd had only one look at her baby...Sam and Lisa's baby...and that look had been blurred by tears.

If she'd done what she knew in her heart she should, if she'd insisted on holding the child, she'd have known immediately it wasn't hers, wasn't the baby she'd given birth to.

Now she had to somehow rectify the wrong. She had to take some control over her life, over Kyla's life. She had to take charge of circumstances, instead of waiting and hoping for the best...trying to hide from the worst. She had to fight for the *best*. She had to go back to Sam's house.

The safety of her condo, ninety minutes away, might as well have been on the moon.

She started her car and pulled away from the store in the direction from which she'd just come. Every movement was an effort, as in nightmares when, pursued by a horrible monster, she could move only in slow motion.

A hurricane roared in her ears as she approached the house.

Pushing the brake, stopping her car at the sidewalk, took every ounce of strength she possessed. Then she had to somehow find more to enable her to get out and walk up to the front door.

He met her there, stepping out onto the porch and standing in front of the door, denying her access to his home. He wasn't smiling anymore.

"Who are you and what do you want?" He advanced on her, his brow furrowed, his face dark, and she backed away, stumbling against the side of one of the chairs she'd sat in earlier. He loomed over her. "If this is some kind of a joke, it's not very damn funny. I'm warning you, Marcie Turner, or whoever the hell you are, if you continue to follow me or my daughter, or if you breathe one word of this nonsense to her, you'll wish you'd never heard of either of us."

Every angry word slammed painfully against her heart. She'd expected him to be upset, but she hadn't been prepared for this furious disbelief. She hadn't been prepared for so much venom from the smiling football coach.

A few feet away, off the porch, the sun still shone brightly. A woodpecker drummed in a nearby tree. A car drove by, releasing a burst of music from its radio. Only in the small area of Sam's front porch had the world turned grim and ugly.

Her hands fluttered up to push him back, to allow her to regain her balance and defend herself. He jerked away before she could touch him.

A steel band wrapped around her chest, squeezing the

breath from her. *For Kyla,* she reminded herself. *For your daughter.*

She forced herself to stand straight, to face him, to pull words from her throat. "I haven't been following you. I came by your house for the first time today, because I had to see Kyla. I had to know for sure if the letter was true, if Kyla was my daughter."

Sam glared at her, his eyebrows forming a straight, continuous line. "You need help. Psychiatric help. Believe me, you're not my daughter's mother."

He was only lashing out at her because he was frightened of losing someone he loved. She shouldn't blame him for that. He was fighting for Kyla, just as she was.

But his accusations hurt. She wasn't accustomed to fighting. She wasn't accustomed to having a nice person, someone she'd like under other circumstances, hating her, saying horrible things about her.

She reached behind her, clutching the cold, solid wrought iron of the chair back. "I know my own child. You and I need to talk, to decide what to do, what's the best thing for Kyla."

Sam paced to the front of the porch, then back again to stand before her, his fists clenched at his sides. "The best thing for Kyla would be for you to drop off the face of the earth."

"Maybe," she admitted, the single word coming out a croak. She cleared her throat, lifted her chin and tried again. "Maybe. But that's Kyla's decision. She's entitled to know the truth, then she can choose how to act on it. If she wants me to leave her alone, I will."

"No. It's not her decision. I'm her father. That makes it my decision, and I intend to see to it that she never hears a word of this garbage. I'm going to give you one chance to stop whatever you think you're doing and disappear quietly before I have to call the police."

She flinched at his classification of her as a criminal, someone who needed to be dealt with by the police. But he hadn't called them yet. He must know, deep inside, that she was telling the truth. He *must*.

She retaliated with her own legal threat. "I talked to a lawyer, and he said I could file a petition with the court requesting genetic testing." Her own hands clenched into fists, the fingernails digging into her palms painfully, as she watched the anger swell on Sam's face. "I don't want to do that," she added. "I thought we could work something out."

"Do you really expect me to give serious consideration to a letter you probably typed yourself, and to your ridiculous threat of going to court?" He flung one arm outward. "Go on. Give it your best shot. File all the petitions you want. See if you can find a judge who'll listen to this trash. But in the meantime—" he leaned closer, jabbing a finger toward her "—you stay away from Kyla."

"I can," she whispered, then raised her voice, determined that no one was going to take her child from her a second time. "I can find a judge who'll listen. I've spoken to my mother and Dr. Franklin's nurse, and they're both willing to testify. I don't want to do it that way, but I will. I don't want to disrupt Kyla's life. I don't want to force myself on her."

"Then don't. Stay out of her life. Kyla's not your daughter. She's *my* daughter, and believe me, lady, you and I have never made a child together. My wife gave birth to Kyla. I carried her home from the hospital." He stepped back, shook his head and raked a hand distractedly through his hair. "Why are you doing this? What do you want?"

"I'm doing this because Kyla is my child. I want to be part of her life."

"You want to take her from a father she loves, from her home?" His words were quieter than before, and she saw the glimmerings of doubt and fear in his eyes.

"No, of course not. I want her to be happy. I know she loves you. I have no intention of taking her from you." In spite of her efforts to be strong, she knew that her voice had lost its certainty, that Sam would sense her weakness and take advantage of it. "I just want to be a part of her life. I want her to know I'm her mother."

He sighed and looked away from her. "If you really did have a baby, and that baby died, I'm sorry. But if you think you're going to take Kyla, you better think again." He turned back to her, his hazel eyes blazing. "I want this insanity ended right now. I don't want Kyla to ever find out about you. But if you think for one minute that's going to stop me from calling the police and having you thrown in jail, you're dead wrong. And I'm keeping those pictures and that letter as evidence." He moved closer, so close she could see the tiny lines around his eyes, where a smile used to live. "I'll do whatever it takes to protect my daughter from you."

He whirled away, strode into the house and slammed the door behind him.

Marcie walked stiffly back to her car, away from her daughter's home, where she wasn't welcome, from Sam's cold threat, his assertion that her baby needed to be protected from her.

She'd made a mistake, coming to McAlester and looking them up. She should have made firm, sensible plans. The lawyer she consulted had suggested she let him call first. That was what she should have done. She should never have given in to her impulse and driven by the house.

Her only excuse was that she'd wanted to be certain Kyla really was her daughter before she did anything. But having an excuse didn't change the situation. Her mother had a roomful of excuses for what she'd done, and they didn't change a thing.

She'd taken a step in the wrong direction, and life gave no opportunities for U-turns. The road chosen, whether by deliberation, impulse or accident, had to be traveled. She'd learned that years ago.

The drive home was going to be a long one. And she doubted that even when she got there she was going to feel safe. Her carefully constructed world was crumbling.

When Marcie finally walked into her condo, exhausted to the point of collapse, the light of the answering machine sitting on the kitchen bar seemed to blink a brighter red than she remembered, an ominous, threatening shade of red.

She hesitated for a moment, wanting only to go to bed. If she pressed that button, would she hear more cruel accusations from Sam? Or had he talked to the police and they were calling to warn her away from Kyla?

She made herself cross the room to the answering machine and press the button. Every muscle in her body tensed as she waited for it to rewind and begin to play.

"It's me, sweetheart." Though it was better than she'd expected, nevertheless, Marcie cringed as her mother's overly bright voice grated along her nerves, prickling like a thousand tiny daggers. "Just checking in to say hi and see if you've found out when I'm going to get to meet my granddaughter."

All the tension from the day returned, and anger Marcie hadn't known she possessed burst from its hiding place. It was all well and good for her mother to be so interested in her granddaughter since Marcie had confronted her with the letter. But if she'd been a little more interested thirteen years ago, this nightmare wouldn't be happening. If she hadn't schemed and conspired and lied to get rid of that granddaughter, she'd have her today. Marcie wouldn't have had to go through the grief of thinking her child had died. Kyla wouldn't have spent the past thirteen years living a lie with a stranger who thought he was her father. Marcie wouldn't now be faced with battling that stranger, hurting him and her daughter and herself.

She jabbed at the button to forward to the next message, to rid herself of her mother's voice, her interference.

"End of messages," the machine's computerized voice announced.

Sam hadn't called. The police hadn't called.

The next move was hers.

She sank onto one of the stools. It had only been a short time ago that she sat at that bar, poring over pictures of a blonde girl, afraid to hope, afraid to let herself be happy, afraid to believe this could really be her child. Now it would seem she'd found her child and lost her in a remarkably short space of time, shorter than before. She'd had nine months before she lost her last time.

Briefly she wondered whether she should take Sam's advice, leave her daughter alone, knowing she was happy. Would that be the loving thing to do? She and her child both had lives...good lives...without each other. For almost thirteen years, each of them had been unaware of the other's existence.

Moving woodenly, she rose and went to the refrigerator to get a glass of iced tea.

When she lifted it to her lips, the taste recalled the glass of tea Kyla had given her, the thrill of sitting on the porch, looking at and listening to the child she'd thought dead.

She sipped the drink slowly, wanting to draw out the taste, the flavor of the memories it evoked.

There was no going back. Now she knew her daughter was out there. She'd seen her, talked to her, drunk tea with her. Maybe Sam would do whatever it took to keep her from her daughter, but she'd do whatever it took to get to her. Kyla had the right to know the truth, and only Kyla had the right to order her to stay away.

She stood silently in the kitchen, running her fingers over the smooth, polished wood of the breakfast bar, looking around, trying to find the secure, content feeling her home usually gave her.

Soft silvery carpet stretched across the living room, interrupted by the muted pastels of her sofa and chairs and the rich wood of her coffee and lamp tables. When she moved in four years ago, she'd decorated with comfort and serenity in mind. Since that time, she hadn't changed anything, hadn't added a picture or moved a piece of furniture.

Every time she opened the door, she knew exactly what to expect.

She'd organized her entire life that way—dependable and safe.

Except suddenly that safety was slipping away.

Her home looked different, somehow. Or maybe it only felt different.

On Monday she'd go to work in the same office with the same people she saw five days a week…seven during tax season. She'd dress the same way she always dressed. She'd tie her hair back the way she always did. She'd get a cup of coffee and go to her desk and turn on her computer…and nobody would know that her whole world had changed.

Marcie crossed her living room to her bedroom, then stopped and looked back at the faint footprints in her carpet.

Just walking through the room had changed it. How much more of an effect would her daughter and Sam have on her life?

It was too late. She wouldn't go back even if she could.

But going forward was damn scary.

Sam sat in his van, elbow on the open window, directly in front of the entrance to the Little Dixie Cinema. His gaze darted back and forth as he alternately checked the door for his daughter, and every car that went past, every movement in the shadows where the streetlights didn't reach.

He'd arrived half an hour early to wait for the movie to end, for Kyla and Rachel to come out.

That woman had him on his guard, edgy, afraid to take any chances that the girls might leave early and she or someone she'd hired might kidnap them. He'd been lucky when she returned for her pictures and letter. Kyla and Rachel had been off somewhere riding their bikes.

But he couldn't count on that kind of luck every time.

He drummed his fingers nervously on the side of his van. Man, the crazies were everywhere, even here in this town he'd always thought of as a refuge from such things. That woman, Marcie Turner—if that was really her name—must be a loony. At first, she'd seemed normal, except for being a little shaken up over the accident. He'd even liked her—been attracted to her, as a matter of fact.

But it wasn't normal to fixate on a kid to the point where she probably really believed that kid—his kid—was her daughter.

The whole damned thing scared him.

Losing somebody you loved could happen so fast, like a giant sword suddenly flashing down and cutting away part of your soul. Like Lisa. One day she was alive and happy, and then she was gone.

He wasn't going to lose Kyla, certainly not to some sick woman, not after his daughter had overcome such gigantic odds to be with him in the first place. After the initial fatal diagnosis on the night she was born, subsequent tests had shown Kyla's heart to be strong and healthy. She was a miracle.

A miracle he'd never questioned.

Before tonight.

He shivered, even as the hot, muggy evening squeezed against him. With a hand that shook slightly, he wiped perspiration from his upper lip.

Of course, miracles weren't logical, he assured himself. That was why they were called miracles. You didn't question them; you just accepted them and gave thanks.

The doors of the theater opened, and the Saturday-night crowd of couples and kids burst out.

When he finally spotted Kyla and Rachel, he realized he had lifted himself off the seat in his anxiety to locate them. One hand clutched the steering wheel, the other arm pressed painfully on the open window.

He forced himself to relax. He couldn't let Kyla or Rachel see him this stressed.

Giggling and talking, the girls dashed over. Kyla yanked open the side door, and they climbed into the back.

And Sam's heart stopped. An Oklahoma panhandle dust storm seemed to pound through his brain, obscuring reason, turning ordinary objects and people into unrecognizable, nightmare figures.

Kyla had loosened her hair from her usual ponytail, and for just a moment he saw Marcie Turner's hair, Marcie Turner's face, superimposed over Kyla's. For a stark, terrifying moment, he knew why Marcie had looked so familiar. She was an older version of Kyla, right down to the small, almost unnoticeable dimple in her chin.

He faced forward, refusing to look at the frightening phenomenon, focusing instead on Kyla's familiar voice, her familiar laughter.

"Dad, are you listening to me?"

"What? Of course I am."

Kyla heaved a dramatic sigh. "No, you're not. You're still thinking about that blond babe I crashed into this afternoon, aren't you?"

She'd called that one right.

"I guess I'm going to have to find him a girlfriend. I mean, it's like the man's a monk."

"If it's all the same to you, I think I'll pick my own girlfriends." *Preferably someone sane.* "At the moment, you're the only woman I have room in my life for."

"Well, okay, but you're not getting any younger, and I don't know how much longer I can be responsible for taking care of you." She and Rachel giggled at that comment.

Smiling to himself, Sam turned the key and started the van. Of course Kyla was his and Lisa's daughter.

What was the matter with him, letting himself buy into Marcie Turner's fantasy?

"Can we get pizza?" Kyla asked as he pulled into traffic. "That's what I asked you when you were ignoring me. Not answering counts the same as if you'd said yes, you know."

It was Sam's turn to heave a dramatic sigh. "Like I ever refuse you anything. I think there may be a law against spoiling a kid as badly as you're spoiled."

Kyla leaned forward between the seats and gave him a loud kiss on the cheek. "I promise not to turn you in if we can have an extra large double-pepperoni pizza."

"Oh, that's great! My kid's learned how to blackmail! That'll look so good on your résumé." He dared a glance at her impish face in the rearview mirror, searching desperately and vainly for Lisa's features, not Marcie Turner's.

Lisa had been a short brunette with dark hair and brown eyes. His coloring was dark, also, but blond hair and blue eyes were recessive traits. They could have sprung from some long-forgotten ancestor. Coloring didn't prove a thing.

When Kyla was a baby, Lisa's family had said she looked like Lisa, and his family had said she looked like him. He and Lisa had agreed that she looked like a baby, period.

Now she looked like a blond twelve-year-old, period. Not like Lisa, but not like Marcie. Okay, so Marcie Turner had the same silky hair, though the shade was a little darker, as if she didn't get out in the sun much. So she had the same thin, straight nose, perfect oval face, wide blue eyes. None of that proved a thing. Lots of people had those traits.

Blood type. That was what mattered. With all the medical tests, he knew Kyla's blood type. O positive, the same as Lisa's.

His world shifted back into focus. The familiar highway, lined with stores, restaurants and gas stations, suddenly became a thing of beauty. The neon signs were works of art.

Let that woman try to take them to court. If by some fluke she succeeded, he'd explain to Kyla that Marcie Turner was a disturbed person and it would be easiest to submit to the genetic blood testing and get it over with. Prove to her that Kyla was *not* her daughter. Maybe then she'd go away.

He pulled into the pizza parlor parking lot. "One super-duper giant pizza with double anchovies coming up!" he announced.

"Daaaad…" Kyla groaned.

She was growing up. A few years ago, she'd have argued with him that she hated anchovies and wanted pepperoni.

He slid out of the van and caught up with the girls as they came from the other side of the vehicle. He shoved his hands into the pockets of his blue jeans, resisting an urge to hug his kid in public, an action he knew would embarrass her.

When they reached the door, he held it open with one hand, but succumbed to the urge to drape the other arm over Kyla's shoulders as she went past him. He needed to touch her, reassure himself that she was still there.

She turned to him briefly, flashing him a quick smile.

And in the light from the pizza parlor, he saw Marcie Turner's face, clearly and undeniably.

For a moment, he stood frozen in place, unable to move, and Kyla walked away from his embrace, from him.

He'd been kidding himself. O positive blood was the most common type. That simply meant she could be Lisa's daughter, not that she definitely was.

Only genetic testing could prove parentage for certain.

And he'd changed his mind about allowing that. He'd fight Marcie Turner to the death to prevent that test.

Chapter Three

Marcie pulled into the parking lot of the Holiday Inn in McAlester. Sam had called late last night and asked—ordered—her to meet him this morning to talk.

He'd been gruff, angry—frightened? She would be in his position.

I don't believe you, he'd said. *I want you to know that. I just don't want any trouble for my daughter.*

What he'd said didn't matter. He did believe her, or he wouldn't have asked her to meet with him.

During the hour-and-a-half drive down, she'd alternated between soaring ecstasy and black, subterranean despair.

It was going to happen. She was going to make contact with her daughter.

Would her daughter like her? Would Kyla hate her for not being determined enough to claim her as a baby?

Would Sam pass along his antagonism to Kyla, make her hate this woman intruding into their lives?

She slid from her car and spotted Sam across the lot. He must have been waiting for her.

He stepped down from the van and strode toward her, his scuffed cowboy boots making firm, determined contact with the solid concrete of the parking lot. His faded jeans were molded to the well-defined muscles of his thighs, and the sleeves of his denim shirt, rolled up to his elbows, accentuated strong forearms.

An unexpected surge of attraction coursed through Marcie, taking her completely by surprise. Astonished and dismayed by her inappropriate reaction, she shoved the feeling aside.

Sam Woodward was handsome, in a rugged sort of way. He definitely had a tantalizing, masculine appeal. But she couldn't afford to let anything sidetrack her right now.

And Sam had the potential to do that. He was more than a little unsettling. He presented the picture of a man securely in charge. That was the last thing she needed. She was struggling to regain control of her life, to straighten out all the problems that had occurred because she'd lost it. As things stood, she was going to have to fight Sam for that control. She needed every advantage; she didn't dare lose the slightest edge.

Sam had his own agenda, and it didn't even come close to matching hers. If she didn't have so much at stake, she'd run from the man as fast as she could.

She straightened her shoulders and went to meet him instead.

"Thank you for agreeing to talk," she said, striving for an amicable beginning.

"You didn't give me much choice."

"I wasn't given *any* choice when my daughter was taken from me." As soon as she said the words, Marcie bit her lip, wishing she could recall them. So much for an amicable beginning. She'd intended to take charge of the discussion, to be reasonable, to keep things on an intellectual level, and already she'd slipped, let her emotions invade.

Sam didn't reply, but she knew his guard had gone up.

She swallowed hard and forced herself to speak the appropriate words. "I'm sorry. I shouldn't have said that."

He nodded, unresponsive, his eyes focused straight ahead. Together, but miles apart, they entered the motel lobby.

"Food smells good." She strove for some sort of conversation to break the thick tension surrounding them as they approached the dining room.

"Yes," he agreed. "They have good food here."

But when they were seated at a square, white-clothed table in the middle of the crowded room and the waitress came to take their order, Marcie asked only for coffee, and Sam seconded the request.

"My stomach's in knots," she admitted, turning her glass of water nervously.

One corner of his mouth quirked upward in a way that almost resembled a weak smile. "Mine, too."

Her gut unclenched a notch. She had to keep in mind that this was just as traumatic for Sam as it was for her.

She cleared her throat and plunged in. "So where's...Kyla?" She made herself say the name, not refer to her as *my daughter*, not throw the issue at Sam the way she'd like to.

"At church."

"She went alone?" For a fleeting moment, she felt guilty that, because of her, Kyla had to go to church without her father. Without *Sam*, she corrected herself.

"No, with a friend."

A friend? Marcie's heartbeat skipped erratically, remembering Kyla's flippant comment about being grown up and dating and making Sam a grandfather. Had she completely missed her daughter's childhood?

"A girlfriend?" She choked out the question.

He scowled. "Of course a girlfriend. What did you think? She's only twelve."

Marcie felt heat rise to her face...embarrassment that she knew so little about her daughter, relief at Sam's words, and irritation at his tone, his superior knowledge of her daughter.

The waitress returned with thick mugs filled with steaming coffee.

Marcie sipped desperately, her attention fixed on the black liquid, a welcome distraction from the man sitting across from her. She wasn't doing this well. She needed to lead the conversation and the decision of what to do next, to ensure that things turned out right this time.

"What do you want?" Sam suddenly demanded, snatching from her any last vestige of control over the situation.

She looked up from her coffee, refusing to back down from the anger in his dark gaze. "To be a part of my daughter's life. To be her mother."

"You want to take Kyla away from me."

The statement fell between them like a weight.

"I told you, I don't," Marcie said. "To be honest, I wish I could. I wish I could turn back the clock and take her from you before you ever held her in your arms. But I can't do that. I've lost almost thirteen years of my daughter's life. I'll never see her take her first step or hear her first word. I won't get to play Santa Claus for her or hide Easter eggs. There's no way I can ever get any of that back."

Sam's eyes darkened even more as she spoke. He wrapped big, capable hands around his coffee cup. His knuckles stood out white against his tan. The tendons bulged all the way up his forearms. For a moment, she thought he might crush the thick mug.

"If there were any way for me to take back my daughter without hurting her," she went on, "I'd do it. If I had any evidence that you were a bad parent, I'd do my damnedest to get her away from you. But as far as I can tell, you're a loving father, and she's happy. And more than I want to have her with me, I want her to be happy."

She'd faced that reality already, but putting it into words, hearing herself admit that she'd never really have her daughter, filled her with a bleak sense of loss.

It was all well and good for Dr. Franklin to beat his breast and repent his actions, but the past couldn't be undone. She and Kyla were the ones who had to live with the results of those actions.

She and Kyla and Sam.

She looked down at the table, swallowed hard, picked up a spoon, then laid it back down.

This whole situation was difficult enough without factoring in the effect it would all have on Sam.

Except there was no way to get around it. She couldn't turn back time. Sam was inextricably linked with Kyla. The three of them were bound together in a tangled web, everyone's fate interdependent on the others'.

"Kyla and I have a special relationship," Sam said quietly. "Since my wife died, I've been mother, father and best friend to her. She *is* a happy kid. Anything you do will only upset her. If you really believe she's your daughter, if you really want the best for her, then go away. Leave us alone."

She met his open, straightforward gaze again and lifted her chin. "No."

"I didn't think you would," he admitted.

"Would you, if you were me?"

They stared at each other in silence across the small table.

The waitress reappeared, poured fresh coffee, then left.

Though the air-conditioning in the restaurant was chilly, Sam's brow shone with perspiration. "You can't prove she's your daughter."

"Yes, I can. And you know it." She threw out the second assertion half believing, half bluffing. He sat rigidly immovable, only the expression in his eyes betraying that she was right.

One twist in her gut uncoiled.

"Damn it!" He slammed a fist onto the table, sloshing coffee from his cup and making her jump. "How can you come into our lives like this and completely disrupt everything? I've worked hard to build a normal life for Kyla. She was five years old when her mother died. Lisa lived for that child. She spent every minute with her. You talk about losing a baby you saw only once. Do you have any idea what it was like for Kyla when she lost her whole world and was too little to understand what had happened?"

Marcie steeled herself against the plea in Sam's dark eyes, even as she blinked back her own tears at the thought of her daughter's pain. "No," she said softly. "I can't imagine that, any more than you can imagine my grief. We've all had terrible things happen, things completely out of our hands. But that's history. We can't change it. All we can do is try to take some control over the future. Agree to the genetic testing," she said challengingly, then held her breath, waiting for his reply.

He shook his head slowly and obstinately. "I love my kid. I won't put her through that."

She refused to rise to the bait, the implication that if she loved Kyla as he did, she wouldn't put her through the testing. "She doesn't have to know anything's going on until it's over. You can tell her it's some test required by the school."

"I've never lied to my daughter."

"Oh? What will you tell her if you talk me into leaving, then one day Kyla discovers the truth and wants to know why you wouldn't let her meet her mother? Will you lie to her then, or tell her the truth?"

Sam flinched almost imperceptibly, and she knew she'd scored a point, even though he promptly denied it. "You're not her mother."

"The only way you'll ever know for sure is to have the test."

He glared at her for a long, tension-filled moment, then shook his head. "If I do, what then?"

At least he hadn't refused outright. "If the genetic testing shows she isn't my daughter, I'll offer my sincere apology for all the trouble I've caused, then walk out of your life, and you'll never hear from me again. But if she is, I expect to be a part of her life."

"How?" he demanded, his voice low, but deep with fury. "Again I'm asking you, what do you want? What do you want from my daughter? And I don't give a damn what any lab test shows. She's *my* daughter. *I've* raised her for almost thirteen years. *I* helped her take her first step. Her first word was *Daddy,* and she said it to *me.* I played Santa Claus for her and hid Easter eggs in the backyard. When she was five years old, I had to break the news to her that her mother was dead. She cried in *my* arms. Just where do you think you're going to fit into this relationship?"

Marcie flinched with each painful thrust. For all those years, she'd believed her baby was dead. Now she'd found her, and for the past two days, she'd had her—in her heart, if not her arms.

Now this man was trying to take her baby away from her for the second time, take her away as surely as he'd walked out of the hospital with her almost thirteen years ago, leaving Marcie with an empty womb and empty arms—an empty life.

She wanted to cry. She wanted to turn the table over on Sam Woodward, then kick him viciously while he was down...the way he was doing to her.

She bit her lip and reminded herself that she had to remain calm. Maybe it didn't feel like it, but she'd gained a lot of ground. She couldn't afford to give in to emotions and risk losing that ground.

"I don't know exactly how I'll do it," she said. "I just know I will. I hope we can work that out between us, two people who have Kyla's best interests at heart. But if we can't..." She hesitated and took a deep breath. "If we can't, the court will."

Defeat showed on Sam's face and in the almost unnoticeable slump of his shoulders. Marcie had won another small, bitter victory.

He lowered his head, plowed his fingers through his tousled brown hair and mumbled something she couldn't understand.

"I'm sorry, I couldn't hear what you said."

He looked at her then, his eyes glittering as dark and forbidding as the waters of a bottomless lake on a moonless night. "I said, all right. We'll take your test, but in the meantime, I want you to stay away from Kyla. I don't want her to know about any of this unless she has to. She's used to having tests regularly, because of that diagnosis of a bad heart when she was born. I won't lie to her, but I won't tell her everything." His square jaw firmed and his lips thinned. "Unless I have to."

Marcie gave a single nod of agreement. Her exultation

at this giant stride toward regaining her daughter was tempered by sadness that Sam Woodward, a decent guy who was on the same side as she—Kyla's side—had to suffer.

"I'll stay away until we get the test results, but I want it scheduled immediately," she said firmly, shoving aside her sympathy. "I have a client who's a doctor at a hospital in Tulsa. I'm sure he can arrange for both of you to come in after hours or on Saturday, if that will be more convenient."

"What's wrong with using the hospital here in McAlester?"

"Nothing," she admitted, though it seemed to her there was a lot wrong with it. Nothing he'd understand, however. She couldn't very well explain to him her fear that when events in her life were taken out of her immediate control, everything went wrong. She'd have to come up with a reason that would appeal to his interests. "If you don't want anyone to know about the tests until the results are final, I'd say you have a lot better chance in Tulsa than here."

He studied her for a minute, his eyes narrowing speculatively. "I'd feel better if we used one where nobody knew either of us. How about Muskogee?"

He didn't trust her...and she didn't blame him. She hadn't wanted the test done at a hospital where he had any influence. "Very well. Neutral territory. I'll make the arrangements."

"You make the arrangements for you, and I'll make them for my daughter and me."

Marcie had to remind herself that Sam wasn't being unreasonable, that she'd probably react the same way if she were in his place.

The first time her detective showed her Sam's picture, she'd liked him immediately. He'd exuded an open, carefree charm. However, the grim, defensive man before her bore little resemblance to the smiling photographs, or to the solicitous man she'd met yesterday. She'd brought pain and uncertainty into his life. She was making an enemy of someone she'd have liked to have for a friend.

She couldn't fault him for his attitude, but neither could she back down.

"That's not the way it needs to be done," she stated. "We'll all three have to have blood drawn at the same lab. They'll compare Kyla's DNA to yours and to mine. We need to find a doctor to order the tests and interpret the results."

Sam drained his coffee and set the cup down on the table...hard enough to make Marcie jump. "Then I'll contact a doctor and let you know."

Marcie fought back the helpless sensation that came as decisions affecting her were once again being taken away by someone else. "Soon?" she pressed. She considering setting a time limit, threatening to go to court if he didn't comply.

But she couldn't bring herself to be that cold. She'd won.

She should leave this proud man his dignity. If he didn't contact her within two weeks, then she could push him. However, she didn't think that would be necessary. She sensed that Sam was an honorable man, and he'd given his word.

Sam slid his chair back and stood, took out a worn leather wallet and tossed money on the table for their coffee. "Damn straight it'll be soon." He glared down at her. "I want this over with fast. And in the meantime, I don't want to see you at our house, or anywhere near Kyla."

Marcie's hands clenched into fists. She'd refrained from throwing the last punch, but he'd given in to the impulse. She nodded agreement, afraid she'd lash out at him if she opened her mouth.

He walked away.

Marcie ordered herself to relax, to understand Sam's anger for what it was...fear of losing the child he loved.

Suddenly, as if she were tuning in to his fears, suffocating doubts overwhelmed her.

What if Sam was right? What if her instincts were somehow wrong? What if Kyla wasn't her daughter? What if she had to lose her child all over again?

She studied his broad, straight back as he walked through the restaurant, with a stride that was still determined, if not quite as confident as when he crossed the parking lot toward her. He was big and strong with a football coach's body—well trained and ready for action. She could easily imagine him comforting Kyla when she was sick or had a bad dream, teaching her to play softball, fighting anyone who might try to harm her...yet he was helpless in this struggle. She could imagine that he must be frustrated and frightened.

As if he felt her gaze on him, Sam turned in the doorway and looked at her.

Across the crowded room, against all logic, she felt a bond flow between them. Irrationally, she wanted to go to him, take him into her arms and comfort him, let him comfort her.

For their fears were the same.

Sam arrived at the Muskogee Regional Health Center a few minutes before six o'clock. Visitors and nurses hurried up and down the hall, but the waiting room on the third floor was deserted except for Marcie. They'd agreed to meet with the doctor together, to receive the news of the genetic testing at the same time.

The past three weeks of waiting had been torture. His emotions had run the gamut from dead certainty that Kyla was his daughter to dead certainty that she was Marcie's. He'd cursed Marcie, then felt compassion for her, wished her off the face of the earth, then experienced an odd desire to see her again, to revive this strange connection between the two of them.

Marcie looked up as he entered the room, the delicate features of her face drawn and pale, her large blue eyes ringed by dark circles. She was dressed in a beige suit, blouse and shoes, as if the subdued color and style could mask her tenseness. Beneath the soft fabric of her blouse, her rounded breasts rose and fell in a jerking, ragged rhythm with each breath.

She perched rigidly on the edge of one of the brown vinyl chairs, her long, slender legs pressed tightly together. The knuckles of both hands were white as they clutched a beige purse in her lap.

''Dr. Langstrom hasn't arrived yet,'' she said, her words straining with taut emotion, in spite of her monotone.

He tried to find the outrage he'd felt the first couple of times he saw her, but it was difficult when she looked so vulnerable, when her worried expression mirrored his own feelings.

He nodded and took a seat in one of the uncomfortable, chairs across from her. ''I'm a little early.''

She gave him a tight smile. ''Me, too.''

He picked up a well-thumbed magazine from the lamp table next to his chair and leafed through it, the pages a meaningless blur.

''It's been a long three weeks.'' She sounded tentative, as if unsure whether she was doing the right thing, offering to share this nightmare experience.

''Yeah, it has been. Long and rough.'' He accepted her offer, resisting an impulse to go to her, wrap her in his arms, assure her that everything was going to be all right.

The strange urge, he told himself, was only because the scene was eerily reminiscent of the times he and Lisa had waited like this, in other hospitals, for Kyla's test results.

Reminiscent, but not the same. Today, no matter what the news from the doctor, there'd be no mutual celebration afterward. Today, only one of them would leave the hospital happy.

"I, uh..." He wiped his damp palms on his blue jeans. *I, uh, what? I hope you lose?* She'd kept her word and stayed away from Kyla, but he'd talked to her on the phone several times and found her to be a reasonable, if determined, woman. Much as he'd like to hate her for what she was putting him through, he found that he couldn't. She was going through her own torment.

A tall, thin man holding a file folder and wearing a white doctor's coat walked briskly inside the door, and Sam shot to his feet as he recognized the doctor who'd ordered the lab work for them.

"Dr. Langstrom!" Marcie exclaimed, her voice seeming an octave higher than normal.

"Ms. Turner. Mr. Woodward." He greeted them brusquely. "Come with me, please."

This was it. The moment of truth.

Sam followed him on legs gone numb. If only his brain and his heart could achieve that same feat.

The doctor led them around the corner to a small, empty office, flicked on the light and went inside.

Sam took a seat in front of the metal desk, next to Marcie, his gaze carefully averted from her. He couldn't stand to see her hopes and desires and fears. He couldn't feel empathy for her right now. He had to focus all his thoughts on somehow making the test results come out in his favor—Kyla's favor.

Langstrom opened a file, settled half glasses on his nose

and studied the contents. "According to the lab results of the tests you ordered," he said without looking up, "there's a 99.2 percent probability that Marcie Turner is Kyla Woodward's biological mother, and less than one percent probability that Sam Woodward is her biological father."

The room around Sam shimmered out of focus. Bone-chilling cold enveloped him, roaring through his head and prickling his skin with a thousand icy needles.

Less than one percent probability that Sam Woodward is her biological father.

Kyla was not his daughter. She'd been born to the stranger sitting next to him, a woman he hadn't known existed a month ago.

Chapter Four

It was true.

With a few words, the doctor had confirmed Marcie's highest hopes and her deepest fears.

In a diner down the street from the hospital, she sat across from Sam, her hands wrapped around a barely warm cup of untouched coffee while her arms rested on the cold Formica table.

Kyla was her daughter.

It was wondrously, incredibly, frighteningly true.

Across the table, Sam stared down at his cup. He'd drunk the contents in hurried gulps, as if the activity allowed him to avoid speaking.

After getting copies of the report, she'd asked Sam to go with her to the restaurant to talk. There was so much they needed to discuss, but in the fifteen minutes they'd been sitting there, neither of them had uttered a word other than to order coffee.

"I guess I knew all along," he finally said, still gazing at his empty cup. His voice came out low with defeat, his big shoulders slumped, and Marcie's victory was not as sweet as it should have been.

He lifted a haggard face. The lines at the corners of his eyes seemed to converge inward, pinching his face, instead of spreading outward like sunbursts. "Deep inside, I knew it from the minute I read that letter. When I threatened you and accused you of being nuts, I knew it then, but I was trying so hard not to admit it to myself, like if I ignored it, I could somehow make it go away."

It was, she thought, as close to an apology as she could expect under the circumstances. Not that she needed an apology for his behavior. "It's okay. I'd have done the same thing if I'd been in your position." She'd won. She could afford to be magnanimous.

"What about her...your lover?"

She didn't blame him for not wanting to give Mitch the label of *father*. "The sperm donor," she said dryly. "Mitch Randall. He was high school class president. He lettered in basketball, football, baseball and track. He was the golden boy, and I was the girl from the wrong side of town. I was very flattered that he wanted to go out with me." Her gaze shifted slightly out of focus, through Sam and into her past, examining her naiveté with amazement.

"Anyway," she continued, "I wasn't really surprised when he refused any responsibility for the baby. Not that I asked him to take any. I always thought of her as mine, not his. He was on his way to college, and he wasn't going to let anything stand in the way of having a good time. He drank too much, partied too much, and died in a car wreck his junior year in college." She recited the facts as if she were talking about a stranger. And she was. She hadn't known him at all.

"I'm sorry."

"It was a terrible waste of talent."

Sam was silent for a few moments, staring at the table-top. Finally, he sat upright, draping his arm along the back of the vinyl-covered booth and thrusting his chin forward. "So what happens now?"

We tell Kyla! she wanted to shout. *I reclaim my baby.*

But of course it wouldn't be that simple. Her baby was gone, replaced by a twelve-, almost thirteen-year-old girl who adored the man who'd raised her.

Her baby was gone and, she realized, so was Sam's. Before she could reclaim her child, she had to return his. She found herself strangely reluctant to do so. She'd mourned Jenny for all those years, visited her grave, talked to her, cried for her and loved her. She couldn't just give her up, no matter how much her mother's heart yearned for Kyla.

"Would you like to visit Jenny's grave with me?" she asked, offering to share. It was, after all, what she would ask Sam to do with Kyla.

"What?" He looked puzzled.

"My— Your— The other baby. The one who died." She swallowed hard, then forced herself to say the words, to give to him what he would have to give to her. "Your daughter."

He looked at her and blinked. Slowly, awareness entered his eyes. That aspect had obviously never occurred to him. He looked beaten. Two deadly blows, losing two daughters, in such a short time would be too much even for a strong man like Sam.

"She's dead," he said quietly. "Lisa's and my baby. She's dead."

Marcie reached across the table and laid her hand on his. The large bones, the slightly rough texture of his skin, were such a harsh contrast with the turmoil on his face. He didn't acknowledge her touch, but he didn't pull away either.

"I named her Jennifer Nicole," she said. "She's buried in Hillsdale Cemetery, under a big oak tree." Unexpectedly, tears filled her eyes, tears for Jenny and for Sam and for the nearly thirteen years of her daughter's life that she'd lost.

"Boy." Sam's eyes were suspiciously bright. "You ever heard that football cheer? *Hit 'em again, hit 'em again, harder, harder?* That's how I feel right now, like I've been punched in the gut by a two-hundred-fifty-pound linebacker, then run over by the whole damn football team. Kind of like the way I felt when the doctor came back from surgery to tell me Lisa wasn't going to make it."

The waitress checked their cups and refilled Sam's.

He moved his hand from Marcie's, picked up the steaming beverage and drained it, then flinched. He set the cup down and looked at it.

"It burns," he said, as if talking to himself. "I can handle that. I understand physical pain. I deal with it every day. I push my boys to work out till it hurts. I push myself even harder, just to show them it can be done. Some nights when I go home, I ache all over. I take a couple of aspirins and put ice on the worst places, and it goes away." He lifted his gaze to hers. "Aspirins and ice aren't going to make this go away."

"Mr. Woodward— Sam—" Somehow the formal title seemed inappropriate after the intimacies they'd just been thrust into. "I told you, I'm not planning to take Kyla from you. I don't want to do anything to upset her. I just want to be her mother."

He frowned, his lips thinning. "You think that's not going to upset her, finding out her whole life's a lie? The man she loves isn't her father, Lisa wasn't her mother? What about Lisa's parents? Kyla's their only grandchild, the only part of Lisa they have left."

Alarm bells went off in Marcie's head. She'd thought they'd be able to work out something between the two of them, two people with Kyla's best interests at heart. Now it sounded as if he were trying to talk her out of establishing her rightful relationship with her daughter.

A moment ago, she'd sympathized with him, felt a bond between them, a linking by virtue of their common losses, the two children they inadvertently shared. With only a few words, he'd severed that bond, put her on her guard.

She had to pull back, keep a safe distance between them.

There was too much at stake here. Caring about people, letting them into her life, gave them power over her. All the people she'd cared about had betrayed her—Mitch Randall, her mother, Dr. Franklin. She'd trusted them, and they'd taken advantage of that trust to make her decisions, to control her life.

No more. She had a goal now, to regain her daughter, and she wasn't about to give Sam even a trace of power in this enterprise.

"She may be their only grandchild, but she's my child," she said, clasping her hands together tightly. "This isn't like an adoption where the birth mother suddenly changed her mind. Nobody asked me what I wanted. I never consented to giving up my daughter. I'm willing to work with you to make this as easy as possible for Kyla, but I want to be a part of her life. Soon."

"Soon." Sam repeated the word as if he didn't understand the meaning. "How? You want me to take you home with me tonight and say, 'Kyla, meet your new mother'?"

Marcie shifted uncomfortably in the cold vinyl booth. "No. Of course not. We should talk to her. I don't know. I haven't thought about how to do it. All I've been able to think about is having my daughter back."

"You said you weren't going to take her away from her home, from me," he said accusingly.

"I'm not," she snapped, frustrated by the problems, the obstacles that should have disappeared with the results of the test. "Maybe we can share custody, like divorced parents do. I swear I'm not going to kidnap her or something. As much as I love Kyla, as desperately as I want to be with her, the thought of suddenly having her all alone terrifies me. I love her because she's my daughter, but I don't know anything about her as a person. I have no idea how to be a mother, especially to a twelve-year-old."

Even as she said the words, Marcie worried that she'd revealed too much of herself, given Sam too much ammunition to use against her. She'd just told this stranger more than she'd told anyone for the past thirteen years. And, of all the people she knew, he was the one she should guard against most carefully.

She wrapped both hands around her cup and wished the waitress would remove the cold coffee and bring her some hot, something she could draw some warmth from.

They stared at each other for several moments, the small table as vast as a battlefield. Sounds and scents skimmed past, as if coming from another world and moving on...of clattering dishes, clinking silverware and people talking, odors of French fries and hamburgers.

"All right," Sam finally said, the words riding out on a long sigh. "But we need to plan this. I think you and Kyla need some time to get to know each other before we say anything."

"You want to put off telling her the truth as long as you possibly can."

"Do you have a better idea?"

Marcie studied Sam's sweat-sheened, determined face.

She didn't have a better idea. She didn't have any ideas at all. He was probably right.

Nevertheless, it chilled her to think that once again somebody else was calling the shots with regard to her daughter. She was being silly, she knew, but she couldn't stop the feeling. That was how this whole thing had gone wrong, with other people making decisions for her.

She drew in a deep breath and forced herself to continue, no matter what route she had to take to get to her daughter. "If she doesn't know I'm her mother, I have no part in her life. How is she supposed to get to know me?"

Sam rubbed a hand over the dark stubble on his square jaw, stubble that seemed to have grown in the half hour they were in the diner. "I'll tell her we talked after I found the envelope you dropped, and that I invited you over to the house for dinner. I'll tell her we're...friends."

"Friends." She repeated the familiar word, which sounded suddenly strange, as if from a foreign language. *Friends* with Sam Woodward. She'd liked him when she saw his pictures, liked his rugged, slightly mussed look, the laugh lines around his eyes. He'd seemed the epitome of the all-American guy.

Even though they were at odds now, even though that man had disappeared, leaving in his place a man wearing a tortured, stubborn, almost menacing look, she didn't dislike him. Actually, she couldn't afford to feel anything for him. Yet he was asking her to pretend to be his *friend.*

She shook her head. "No. I don't want to deceive my daughter. There's been too much deception already."

He uttered a quiet but profound oath and leaned across the tabletop toward her. "Deceive her about being friends? If we're going to get through this mess without completely ruining Kyla's life, we'd damn well better figure out some way to be friends, even if we have to grit our teeth to do it.''

She glared at him. ''Not telling her the complete truth isn't right.''

He sat back, running restless fingers through his already disheveled hair. ''Okay, maybe it's not the best plan, but it's the only one I can come up with. I'm willing to listen, if you have a better one.''

Much as she hated the thought of lying, even by omission, she had to admit that Sam's proposed arrangement would give both Kyla and her time to get acquainted, and she didn't have a better plan.

''What if she thinks we're...dating? I mean—'' Marcie could feel the blood rush to her face as she bit off the words she'd been about to say. *You're a man, I'm a woman.* It was an impersonal observation, but somehow the thought didn't feel at all impersonal. Inexplicably, the idea of being a woman around the man who was Sam struck her with a very personal edge.

''I imagine that's exactly what she'll think.'' His lips thinned as he gazed at her unflinchingly. ''You're a beautiful woman, a 'babe,' according to Kyla. We'll just have to deal with that misconception when the time comes.''

He'd thrown her a compliment, then crushed it under his foot. ''Very well,'' she said, trying to match his detached tone. ''When?''

''Saturday evening, five o'clock.''

It was that simple, then. She was going to begin a relationship with her daughter in two days. That was all that mattered. What Sam did or didn't think of her was unimportant.

''We'll grill some hamburgers,'' he continued, ''maybe rent a video, make some popcorn and relax. That's a typical Saturday night for us.''

For us. For Sam and Kyla. She'd be an intruder. An unwelcome intruder on Sam's part, and maybe on Kyla's. For a moment, she panicked. Was she doing the right thing? Certainly, it was unlikely she and Sam would ever be friends. She could stand that. She had no emotions invested in him. But what would she do if Kyla didn't like her, if she lost her daughter again?

She couldn't think about that. She had to try. If nothing else, she had to give her daughter the chance to make that choice.

"I'll be there," she said. "Can I bring something? A bottle of wine? No, I guess that's not appropriate, is it? Maybe dessert or something?"

Sam leaned back, laying both palms flat on the table, as if conceding defeat. "Sure, why not? You could bake a cake. Her favorite is chocolate with chocolate frosting."

Like the sun breaking through storm clouds, Marcie felt a wide, giddy smile spread across her face. She'd just been given a piece of her daughter, her favorite kind of cake— the kind she herself preferred. *Like mother, like daughter.*

"Chocolate cake. Yes, I'll bake a chocolate cake." She'd never baked a cake in her life, but she could learn to do it for her daughter. "Anything else?"

Sam shook his head. "Dress cool. Our house is old. We don't have central air." He slid out of the booth and stood. "Does that conclude our business?"

"I suppose it does." How naive she'd been only a few minutes ago, thinking she and Sam shared a common bond, in their losses, their children. They both wanted the best for Kyla, but their opinions of what constituted that *best* put them on opposite sides.

Sam pulled his wallet from his pocket and started to open it, but she laid her hand on his to stop him.

"You paid for the coffees at our last meeting. It's my turn."

Sam pulled his hand away from her. "No woman I'm with picks up her own check, let alone mine."

The amount of money was inconsequential, and Marcie knew she was overreacting, but suddenly it became important that she assert herself, take control of some element of their meeting. "You're not *with* me, and I'm not a *woman* to you. Like you said, this is a business deal, and buying your coffee is much cheaper than if I had to pay attorneys' fees." She opened her purse and took out her own wallet.

Sam tossed a five on the table, and she did the same.

Marcie rose, and they crossed the restaurant together. They were almost out the door when their waitress's excited voice reached them. "Thank you very much! Y'all come back."

Marcie wanted to giggle. She wanted to look at Sam and laugh and share the way their stubborn acts had inadvertently made a stranger's day.

She squelched the impulse. She'd slipped before and given in to her emotions, let herself be concerned about Sam. She'd almost compromised her position. Sam had said this was strictly a business deal, and she'd agreed with him. There was no place in that assessment for shared laughter.

From behind the steering wheel of his battered van, Sam watched Marcie Turner pull out of the hospital parking lot in her little silver car.

For a few minutes, he'd almost let her get to him, almost been sucked in by the softness of her fingers on his, the vulnerability in her eyes that gave the lie to her sophisticated, confident appearance. For a few minutes, he'd felt a connection between them. For a few minutes, he'd forgotten what Marcie's goal was—to take Kyla from him.

Not that he blamed her. He understood the phenomenon of being a parent. When Kyla was born, Lisa had devoted herself entirely to the baby, obsessed with the only child they'd been able to produce.

And that was the ultimate irony. They hadn't produced Kyla.

Maybe part of Lisa's obsession had sprung from some deep maternal knowledge of that truth. Maybe that had had something to do with the way she clung to Kyla so desperately.

Whatever the source, Marcie had that same focus. She wanted Kyla, all of Kyla, only Kyla.

He wasn't sure how Kyla was going to react to Marcie. He hadn't dated many women since Lisa died. Kyla deserved all his attention, since he was the only parent she had. No woman could, he thought, love a child as much as her own mother had, as much as he did.

Now he found that Lisa had adored her in spite of the fact that she hadn't given birth to her, that he loved with all his heart a child he hadn't fathered. And that child's mother had appeared, a woman who could love Kyla as much as he and Lisa.

He'd been attracted to Marcie the first time he met her, attracted on a primal, man-woman level. One more ironic twist to the situation—the first woman who'd claimed his interest in a long time was the one woman he could never get involved with.

Even if he didn't have to stay on his guard constantly for fear she'd try to take his daughter, he knew her focus was solely on Kyla. She was totally unaware of him as a man. Lisa's obsession with Kyla had been complete, making him feel excluded. How much stronger would it be for Marcie, the woman through whose veins flowed the same blood as Kyla's?

Chapter Five

It was only four-thirty. The minute hand on Marcie's watch seemed to have taken an hour to move from the four to the six, and still it was too early to leave for Sam's house, only ten minutes away.

In order to have time to relax before their meeting and not have to worry about getting sleepy on the long drive home afterward, she'd checked into the motel in McAlester where she'd met Sam for coffee that first time. So far, the *relaxation* part hadn't materialized, and if she stayed this hyped and anxious, she doubted she'd be the least bit sleepy at the end of the evening.

She went into the bathroom and checked her hair, makeup and dress for the thousandth time.

Maybe she ought to change from a dress to slacks, or even shorts.

She'd brought half a dozen outfits with her, unable to decide which would be most appropriate. After checking in, she'd tried them all on at least once, remembering her own teenage years, when clothes—her own, her mother's, everybody's—had been so important.

She surveyed the white cotton sundress critically. Not particularly trendy or stylish, but she didn't have any trendy clothes.

It would be *cool,* as Sam had suggested. But other than that, *nondescript* was the only term she could come up with to describe it.

She checked her watch again.

Ten minutes to five! The dress would have to do. Better that Sam and Kyla find her nondescript than that she be late.

A flush crept over the face that looked back at her from the motel room mirror as she realized that Sam's approval of her clothing had been haunting the outer regions of her thoughts, that he had something to do with her unaccustomed concern about clothing.

Turning away from the mirror, she pushed the confusing reaction aside. She didn't have time to worry about it or deal with it now.

She grabbed her purse and the plastic container containing her chocolate cake and ran out the door.

On the first part of the drive over to Sam's house, she exceeded the speed limit, consumed with anxiety that she'd be late, that Sam would change his mind, that Kyla would get a call from a girlfriend and leave to see a movie.

Then she found herself slowing down below the speed limit, trying and failing to remember the thousand comments she'd rehearsed to say to her daughter.

Suddenly she was there, ready or not.

She sat in her car for a moment, looking at the house, eager and terrified to go in.

Though she always referred to and thought of her modern, private condominium as *home,* it didn't have the same sense of nurturing welcome as this big old two-story frame structure half-hidden by trees.

No matter what happened in the future, she would always be grateful to Sam for giving her daughter a happy childhood. Her mother had achieved half of what she set out to do. Kyla had never known the rented rooms and scanty meals of her own childhood.

She licked her dry lips, climbed out of the car and headed down the sidewalk. Her palm, wrapped around the handle of the newly purchased cake carrier, was damp, and her stomach was clenched into a tight little knot. She hadn't been this nervous when she took her C.P.A. exam.

She hadn't had as much at stake then.

Just as she stepped onto the front porch, Sam opened the door and smiled at her. With the exception of a slight tenseness around the corners of his mouth and eyes, it was the smile she'd seen in his pictures, the smile he'd owned before she came into his life.

It was a captivating smile, and even though she knew it was all pretend, all for Kyla's benefit, her own lips curved upward in automatic response.

"Marcie, come in. I'm so glad you could make it."

He stepped back, holding the door for her, and she saw Kyla peering curiously around him. Her smile widened, elation overwhelming her, even as her insides trembled. This was *it*, the moment she'd been waiting for. Now all she had to do was somehow be charming enough and bright enough and lovable enough to reach her daughter's heart.

Forcing herself to walk on rubbery legs, she crossed the porch toward the open door, toward her baby.

Sam watched Marcie as she walked toward him. The white dress she wore floated about her, touching her sleek curves, then drifting away. Her shiny hair caressed her shoulders, rippling with her every step. For just an instant, when he first opened the door, he'd felt her excitement and happiness as she smiled at him, her face radiant.

Then he'd stepped back and realized Kyla was right behind him.

Of course Marcie's joy wasn't directed toward him. She was here to see his daughter. To try to take his daughter away—physically or emotionally or both.

"Kyla, you remember Marcie Turner?"

"Sure. I never forget people whose cars I run into. Did you ever get that dent fixed?"

"Dent? Oh, uh, no, I haven't. I hadn't really thought about it again. I've, uh, been busy."

She seemed as edgy as she'd been the first time she came by. He'd thought then that she was upset about the softball hitting her car, about almost running into Kyla. But, of course, that hadn't been her problem.

Later, she'd been one cool, determined lady when fighting for the right to see Kyla, but now she was eager and unsure. He remembered her saying she was terrified at the thought of suddenly assuming the role of Kyla's mother. She'd obviously been telling the truth. The suffocating band around his chest loosened a fraction of an inch. Kyla was safe with him for the moment.

"Good thing you didn't drive by when we were practicing skeet shooting."

Marcie whirled to face him, her eyes wide, her full lips slightly parted.

"She's being funny. Trying to be, that is." He grasped Kyla's head in the crook of his arm, the familiar gesture a comfort to him, as well as a warning to Marcie that she wasn't going to intrude between the two of them. He wanted her to be certain where he stood. No matter what the test had shown, Kyla was still his daughter. "All right, demon child, stop terrorizing our guest and let's get the charcoal started."

"Cool! I love doing the fire thing." She darted through the house and out the back door, blond ponytail bouncing behind.

"Should she be lighting a fire?" Marcie asked.

"Been doing it for years. She's twelve, almost a teenager, nearly an adult." He'd made the comment to emphasize to Marcie that Kyla was no baby, that it was too late to step in as her mother, but the moment he saw the pain in her sky-blue eyes, he wished he could take back his words. "According to her, at least," he temporized. "Come on. Let's go out back."

He led the way through the living room and kitchen to the back door. Marcie moved gracefully beside him, the soft fabric of her dress swaying gently with each step. In spite of her nervousness, she projected an innate elegance. The contrast caused Sam to notice the worn area rug in the living room, the scuffed vinyl in the kitchen, the mismatched furniture everywhere. He'd always been comfortable in the old house, but suddenly he wondered how Marcie would view it.

They reached the backyard just in time to see Kyla toss a match onto the waiting charcoal, then jump back before it flared.

Beside him, Marcie gasped and lunged forward, toward Kyla. He grabbed Marcie's arm, restraining her.

"Typical dramatics for a twelve-year-old meeting her father's…date." The smooth skin of Marcie's arm against his palm, the light, clean fragrance of summer rain that drifted from her hair, the alluring curves of her body outlined by the soft fabric of her dress, all made it damned hard to remember that she wasn't really his *date*.

He reminded himself that this was all a game of make-believe that he'd invented for Kyla's benefit, an effort to minimize the shock of Marcie's invasion of their lives. The tantalizing woman beside him was no girlfriend-to-be. Not now. Not ever.

He turned loose of her arm, promising himself he wouldn't touch her again, wouldn't risk losing control to those enticing, disrupting sensations she evoked.

Kyla grinned and sauntered over. "Don't sweat it. I hardly ever catch myself on fire. The house and a couple of trees, but not myself."

Marcie laughed shakily. "Of course. I didn't think..." She looked down, then gave a slight start, as if she'd suddenly noticed the plastic container in her hand. "Oh! Here. Your, uh, *Sam* said you like chocolate cake."

He didn't miss her refusal to refer to him as *your father*.

Kyla gave him a quick, cynical glance. He knew that she grouped the infrequent women he dated into three classifications: those who ignored her, those who wanted to be her best friend, and those who wanted to be her mother.

One mark in the mother category, and a very clumsy one. Usually his dates tried to work in their offerings with a little more subtlety. He should be glad Marcie had made such a faux pas, but, oddly, he wasn't.

"Dad said I like chocolate cake, so you made one for me." Kyla accepted the cake. "How nice. Thank you."

"Well," Sam said, "shall we take that cake inside and get something to drink while the coals burn down?"

"Relax," he whispered, walking closer to Marcie than was probably necessary and feeling anything but relaxed himself as they crossed the yard.

"I can't," she whispered. Her back was rigid and her steps were halting as she went inside.

"Have a seat." He indicated the square wooden table beside the bay window at one end of the large kitchen.

"How about a beer?" Maybe that would calm her down a little. Maybe *he* should have a whole six-pack.

"No, thanks. Water will be fine."

"I made some tea," Kyla contributed, letting the screen door slam behind her.

"Yeah, you put the tea bags in a jug of water and set it in the sun," Sam teased, grateful to have his attention diverted.

Kyla gave him a playful punch in the arm. "You think it's so easy, you do it next time. Want some, Ms. Turner?"

"Yes, thank you. I'd love a glass. And, please, call me—" Sam tensed as her gaze darted frantically from Kyla to him, across the room and back to Kyla. Was she going to ask Kyla to call her *Mother?* That wasn't the kind of gradual working up to the revelation that they'd agreed on. "Marcie," she concluded uncertainly, and he slowly released the breath he'd been holding.

Her strange actions brought a covertly lifted eyebrow from Kyla as she passed him on her way to the refrigerator at the far end of the room.

He needn't have worried about Marcie stealing his daughter. She was doing all the wrong things. She might be a sophisticated lady, a competent accountant, maybe even a social charmer, but with Kyla, she was a fumbling basket of nerves.

And to his surprise and consternation, instead of being glad about her failure to communicate, he ached for her.

He'd expected this evening to be crazy. He'd started out nervous himself, and he'd known it would get worse. But no way had he been prepared for the strange need to console Marcie for her inability to make contact with his daughter, or the heady sensations evoked by being close to her.

"You want tea, too, Dad?"

"Yes, Princess. Thank you."

Kyla chunked ice into three glasses, then returned to the table in the clumsy, graceful way of moving she'd developed just this summer. "You want sugar and lemon, right?" she asked as she poured tea over the ice.

"Plain is fine, thank you," Marcie replied.

"Dad, can I have that beer you offered Marcie? I haven't had any beer in over a month now."

Marcie's eyes became even wider, but before she could say anything, Kyla glanced out the back door. "I think I better go check on my roaring inferno."

"She's kidding," he said softly as the screen slammed behind Kyla. "Preteenage humor is strange."

Impulsively he lifted Marcie's clenched fist from the tabletop and gently straightened her fingers.

She gave him a weak smile. "I'm not doing this very well, am I?"

"You're doing fine," he lied, wondering why he couldn't tell her the truth. He still held her hand. Warm tingles zipped up his arm, catching him off guard, spreading through his body like the ripples from a pebble tossed into a pond on a sultry summer day.

He should turn her loose, but his hand didn't want him to. Her fingers were long and slim and cool beneath his, the kind of fingers that invited a man to stroke and caress.

Kyla charged back inside, and he dropped Marcie's hand as if it were on fire.

Kyla flopped into a chair and spooned too much sugar into her tea, but Sam couldn't seem to find his voice to protest. "I'm getting so good at this fire thing, I may major in arson." She stirred her tea noisily.

Marcie lifted her glass and took a long drink, her gaze avoiding his, as if she could avoid the way he'd held her hand for longer than he should, then dropped it guiltily.

He ought to do the same thing. Ignore it. Ignore the smooth porcelain stretch of her throat as she tilted her head back to drink, the way her silky hair floated onto her shoulders, the way he was fascinated by every move she made.

He clenched his fist at his side. He wasn't doing a very good job of ignoring anything.

Marcie carefully set her tea on the table, still not looking at him. "So, what grade are you in, Kyla?"

He cringed as she asked the question. He refused to look at Kyla, to be even a nonparticipating part of another raised eyebrow.

"I'm in the eighth grade, Marcie. Next year, if Dad bribes enough school officials, I'll be in the ninth."

"Unless Dad beats you so severely you can't sit down long enough to attend class," he growled, then cast a quick glance at Marcie, anticipating another shocked expression.

However, she was smiling...faintly and wistfully, but smiling nevertheless. She'd noticed the easy closeness he shared with his daughter...a closeness she didn't have.

"Really, he doesn't beat me," Kyla assured her. "At least, not very often."

"Really, I imagine Marcie realizes I've never beaten you. If I had, you wouldn't have such a smart mouth."

Kyla shrugged impishly. "Can't help it. I inherited it from you."

Well, Sam thought, *Kyla's reference to heredity should put an end to that conversation.* "Think it's time to go check on those coals again?" he asked pointedly.

"Yes, Father." She giggled before dashing outside.

Marcie lifted both hands to her face and took a deep breath as the door slammed behind Kyla. "I'm a wreck. I don't know what to do or say. This is so hard, being an instant mother."

"Give it some time." To his surprise and chagrin, he

again found himself trying to comfort her. Her pain was so obvious, he couldn't help but feel it, too. "You haven't been around many kids, have you?"

"No, I haven't." She drew a finger through the moisture accumulating on the outside of her tea glass, her eyes intent on the gesture. "After...everything that happened, I avoided children. I didn't want to be reminded."

Sam wished she hadn't told him that. He didn't want to know how vulnerable she was. He didn't want to see her as a real person. He didn't like feeling sympathetic toward her any more than he liked being attracted to her. Both feelings weakened his position.

Kyla burst into the room again. "The coals are ready." She swung open the refrigerator door and pulled out the foil-covered pan of meat patties.

As Marcie watched Kyla, her eyes filled with longing.

"Come on, Marcie," Sam said. "If we're going to eat these burgers, we'd better get outside and keep an eye on the cook." He wasn't going to help her, but he wouldn't deliberately hurt her efforts. That was as far as he could go. If she failed to establish any kind of rapport with Kyla—and she was doing a really good job of failing so far—it wouldn't be his fault.

Marcie finished her burger and leaned back in the lawn chair. "That was good."

She hadn't expected to be able to force even one bite down her tense throat, but, amazingly, she'd eaten, and actually enjoyed it.

Sam's backyard was as homey and inviting as his house, and had a calming effect. They'd dined beneath a huge elm tree that must be at least fifty years old. The long, weathered wooden picnic table couldn't be much newer, and the aluminum folding chairs were all covered in different materials.

The yard, a corner lot, was big, with more clover than grass. The evening sun cast long shadows through the forest of trees. The grill where Kyla had created her conflagration sat several feet away, and Marcie noted that the leaves and branches above bore a scorched look.

Honeysuckle sprawled along what was probably a forgotten remnant of a fence separating their property from the neighbor behind them, but other than that, Sam's yard had no enclosure.

However, the thing that undoubtedly contributed the most to her being able to eat and to actually converse with Kyla was Sam's attitude. From the first time they talked, he'd fought her every inch of the way, taking so much of her emotional energy that every small victory exhausted her. She'd expected him to make her already tense meeting with Kyla unbearably difficult.

Instead, he'd actually gone out of his way to be gracious, to reassure her, to lie to her and tell her she wasn't being as socially inept as she knew she was. She'd had to resist the temptation to fall into the charade they were acting out, that she was Sam's *friend,* that his hand on her arm or holding hers at the kitchen table was more than accidental, casual touching.

But she wasn't his *friend.* She was his worst nightmare. And she didn't dare let his charm lull her into easing her vigilance, losing control of the situation.

"You sure you don't want another burger?" Kyla offered.

"Thank you, no. I'm stuffed. Everything was great."

"You think so? We got the potato salad and coleslaw at the grocery store."

Marcie looked at Sam to see if Kyla was teasing again.

He shrugged and grinned. "We did. I'm not much of a cook, and hamburgers pretty much stretches Kyla's limits."

"Yeah, we usually just have chips with our burgers. But Marcie cooks!" She slid her chair back and burst up from it like a jack-in-the-box. As usual, her movements were in fast forward. "Can we have cake now?"

"Why don't we let our burgers settle for a few minutes?" Sam suggested. "You ate two. Surely that'll hold you for a little while."

"I'm growing, Dad. I need a lot of nourishment."

"Eat another pickle."

"Can I have a cola?"

"If you'll bring us some more tea."

Marcie watched her bound into the house, then turned back to see Sam looking at her speculatively. "She's wonderful," she said.

"Yeah."

At least they agreed on that.

"You've given her a good home," she said quietly.

He looked relieved at that comment, and she realized he was still terrified about whether she would try to take Kyla from him.

"I think she's happy," he said.

"Yes. I can tell she is." It was her turn to offer him reassurance, and in offering that reassurance, she was suddenly aware of how much it must have cost Sam to encourage her. Admitting to him that Kyla was happy was admitting that Kyla didn't need her, that she could live her entire life without knowing Marcie was her mother and never be the worse for it. Sam must have felt something similar when he held her hand and told her she was doing fine, when he encouraged her to *give it some time*.

"I brought the cake, just in case your burgers have settled by now." Marcie looked up to see Kyla holding her plastic container in one hand, the pitcher of tea in the other and a red can of cola cradled in the crook of her arm.

"Let me help you." She scrambled up and took the tea from her.

Kyla set the cake on the table and removed the cover. She hesitated for the space of a heartbeat. "Hey, this looks really good."

Marcie gasped at the transformation her cake had undergone. It was probably the worst one she had ever seen. Not only was it lopsided, with a large crack in the top, one layer had slid halfway off the other, and much of the frosting had puddled around the bottom.

Dismay descended like a heavy black cloud. Why, when it mattered the most, had she changed from a competent professional to a bungling, tongue-tied klutz who couldn't do anything right?

"It didn't look this bad when I left home with it. Everything seems to have shifted. I'm sorry. I don't bake many cakes."

"That's cool," Kyla assured her, poising the knife to begin cutting. "I guess accountants don't have a lot of spare time. Doing tax returns and saving people from the clutches of the IRS is a lot more important than baking cakes." Using the gaping fissure as a guide, she sliced through. "Let the bakers bake and the accountants account."

Her daughter was being kind, and that lifted Marcie's spirits, but Kyla was wrong. No career, no matter how successful, was nearly as important as baking a perfect cake for her daughter.

The first piece crumbled as Kyla slid it onto a paper plate.

"We can't eat that," Marcie protested, in total humiliation. "I saw a Braum's ice-cream place on the highway. Let's go there, my treat."

"Food doesn't have to look good to taste good, does it, Dad? You should see some of the yucky things he cooks up. We had this one casserole that looked like—"

"Kyla! Don't say it. Whatever it is, just don't say it. Otherwise, none of us will want to eat another bite."

"Okay, Pops." Kyla served up two more crumbly slices of the cake and eagerly took a taste. She chewed once, looked at Marcie, chewed a couple more times and swallowed hard, her face contorting.

A few seconds ago, Marcie would have sworn she couldn't be more embarrassed, but now she was. "I knew it. It's terrible, isn't it? I'm sorry. Let's go to Braum's."

Kyla took Marcie's fork, cut off a small piece and offered it to her. Her own daughter was contributing to her humiliation. She accepted the cake tentatively, expecting a vile taste.

Actually, it was pretty good. She swallowed, then took another bite. Excellent, in fact.

Kyla burst into giggles. "Gotcha!" She shoveled in more cake. "So it looks a little funny," she mumbled, talking with her mouth full. "Tastes great. You did a pretty good job, Marcie, especially for somebody with no practice. Next time I'll teach you to make s'mores. They don't take much time, and you hardly ever ruin them."

Marcie's heart soared. The sun had just risen in her life. Not only was her daughter teasing her, but she'd mentioned *next time*. She wanted to see her again.

As the evening progressed, Sam couldn't decide whether Kyla really wanted to see Marcie *next time* or was in her caretaker-for-the-underdog personality.

The three of them sat in his living room, he in his battered, comfortable recliner and Marcie and Kyla on the sofa, and Marcie continued to make every known faux pas in her eagerness to get to know Kyla.

She'd asked about his daughter's plans for the future, her dreams and aspirations, what classes she liked in school, who her friends were, even her height and weight. Kyla had borne it all in amazingly good spirits. Sometimes her flip answers had bordered on sarcasm, but mostly she'd treated Marcie as though their roles were reversed, as though Marcie were the child and she the patient mother.

With the onset of puberty, he'd seen many different facets of his previously uncomplicated little girl, but this was an entirely new one. He had no idea how to gauge her feelings about Marcie. He only knew that the more comfortable Marcie became, the more uncomfortable he became.

Surely Kyla was too bright to fall for the blatant adulation shown her by Marcie. On the other hand, who in her right mind wouldn't fall for blatant adulation?

Marcie laughed at something Kyla said, something adolescent and not particularly funny, something he'd have rolled his eyes and groaned at.

He studied the two of them, sitting side by side, looking so much alike, completely enthralled by their own conversation, and suddenly another aspect of the situation hit him squarely in the chest.

He felt left out.

Just like the evenings with Kyla and Lisa before his wife's death—mother obsessing over daughter, shutting him out, refusing to admit him into a relationship with either of them.

In this case, of course, it wasn't so much being left out of Marcie's focus as being snatched out of Kyla's. He had no reason to feel excluded by Marcie. If he did feel that way, it was just a knee-jerk reaction to similar scenes with Lisa and Kyla.

A feeling of being powerless built steadily as he watched Marcie and his daughter, Marcie and her daughter. He wanted to order Kyla upstairs to bed, but she was too old for that. He wanted to order Marcie to leave. He wanted to be included in the relationship building in front of him. He wanted to hate Marcie for what she was doing.

He couldn't do any of those things.

Finally, Marcie rose to leave.

"Think I'll go on to bed," Kyla said, stretching, then yawning loudly, though she'd shown no signs of being sleepy before that moment.

"Don't you want to walk out to the car with Marcie?"

Kyla rolled her eyes. "Oh, yeah, like the reason Marcie came over here was to spend the entire evening with your daughter." She turned to Marcie. "Be patient with Dad. He hasn't had much experience with women. Night, everybody!"

Marcie stood unmoving, obviously crushed, only a few feet from the door.

"Kyla!" Sam exclaimed. "You're being rude. Marcie is our guest, and we're both going to walk her to her car." He couldn't believe his own ears, couldn't believe he was actually trying to help Marcie's cause. He was such a sucker for that forlorn look.

Kyla gave a dramatic, frustrated sigh. "You all go ahead. I'll come out after you have a chance to, you know, say good-night. I have to go brush my teeth now."

"Brush your teeth?" Marcie repeated.

Sam took Marcie's arm. "When she was little, her grandparents—Lisa's parents—taught her to say that instead of asking to go to the bathroom. They thought it sounded better. Come on. We'll go outside and wait for her."

They walked out into the warm darkness of the summer night.

"Thank you," Marcie said, turning to him, when they reached the end of the sidewalk. "It's been a wonderful evening."

"Yeah, it turned out all right. I have to admit, I didn't really know what to expect, but everything went well."

She smiled. "I wasn't sure what to expect, either. I was pretty nervous."

Sam felt a little nervous himself, unsure what he ought to be feeling right now...unsure exactly what he did feel. He glanced toward the house, expecting to see Kyla burst out the door. Instead, he saw her face peeking around the blinds of the living room window.

"Don't look now, but Kyla's watching us."

"Watching us?" Marcie repeated. "Why? I thought she was coming out to join us."

Sam ran a hand through his hair and gave a short laugh, an embarrassed laugh. "I think she's waiting for us to say good-night."

She looked at him curiously, tilting her head, and the silver moonlight danced in her hair and touched her face, giving her a glow that seemed to come from within.

"To kiss good-night." The words came from far away, from someone else, someone who wasn't embarrassed by his daughter's antics, someone who wanted to kiss the beautiful woman in front of him.

"Oh," she said.

Tentatively, he cupped her face in his hand and leaned toward her, intending to lightly brush her lips with his, to give her the barest imitation of a kiss, just enough to satisfy Kyla. But her scent of summer rain washed over him, blending with the moonlight, as she responded, her satiny lips clinging to his, and whatever he'd intended to do melted in the tantalizing sensation of kissing Marcie.

A cluster of heat that had nothing to do with the August night surged up from his gut, spreading all through him. He heard a soft moan, and wasn't sure if it came from him or her or was only in his mind.

As if moving through quicksand, he forced himself to pull away from her, to step back and catch his breath.

Her lips were parted slightly, ready to be kissed again, and her eyes were wide and startled. He felt himself moving back to her, unable to resist the strong pull, the need to kiss her, to hold her body against his.

The screen door slammed, jerking him back to reality. Kyla was coming out. The kiss had been enough to satisfy her, but it wasn't enough to satisfy him. Whatever had just happened between them was only enough to whet his appetite, to confirm the desires stirred earlier simply by touching her.

"Night, Marcie!" Kyla said, jogging up beside him. "Your cake was really good."

"I'm glad you liked it." Marcie sounded a little breathless, too, but back in control. "I'm spending the night at the Holiday Inn. Would you all like to meet me there for brunch tomorrow? Both of you?"

Sam blinked as Marcie's words hit him like a cold shower. How could he have forgotten so easily? She was here to see Kyla, not him. She'd kissed him so that Kyla would come out. This wasn't about Marcie and him. There would never be a Marcie and Sam. This was about Kyla and him, Kyla and Marcie.

"Go for it, Dad. I can go to church with Rachel tomorrow."

"No," he said. "I haven't been to church with you in several weeks. We're going."

Kyla sighed and shook her head, as if in despair. "Dad, you can really be dense sometimes. Okay, then Marcie can come with us, and we'll all go to brunch after church."

"Thank you," Marcie said, relief evident in her voice. "I'd love to."

Of course she would love to go with them. That was what she was here for. All she was here for.

He draped a protective, possessive arm about Kyla's small shoulders, and they stood at the curb and waved to Marcie as she drove away.

"I like her," Kyla said as they walked back up the sidewalk. "We can see her again."

"You like her?" He stopped in his tracks as Kyla vaulted onto the porch. He'd sensed it, but hearing Kyla put it into words was like a death sentence.

One arm stretched out, she clutched a column with the other and swung around. "Yeah. She's okay. She just needs a little help learning how to be cool. I'll bet she was a real nerd when she was in school. But I think we can help her."

I think we can help her. But who the hell was going to help him? As if he didn't have enough to worry about with the specter of losing Kyla, of her reaction when she discovered the truth about Marcie, he also had to battle his own tangled feelings about the woman who threatened his happiness.

Chapter Six

Marcie loaded her suitcase into her car, checked out of her room then stood in the lobby of the Holiday Inn, waiting for Sam and Kyla to pick her up for church.

A few people passed, coming in, going out, on their way to other places, but they were ghosts, unknown persons she couldn't have identified later if one of them committed murder right in front of her. Her entire scope of vision was concentrated on the parking lot, as she looked for Sam's van.

She couldn't wait to see Kyla again.

At the same time, the thought of seeing Kyla again filled her with terror.

And with Kyla came Sam. Unavoidably.

She didn't know how she felt about seeing him.

For one insane moment last night, she'd let go and let herself get caught up in the make-believe relationship Sam had invented. For that moment, she'd plunged recklessly into the heady sensations his kiss evoked...just as she'd plunged recklessly into her brief relationship with Mitch so many years ago.

Her only consolation was that this time she could explain her foolish reactions. All evening she'd been riding a surge of adrenaline, elated at being with her daughter. It was only logical that some of that excitement would spill over to encompass everything and everyone she came in contact with...and she'd come in contact with Sam's lips.

Marcie shifted her weight from one foot to the other and stared across the parking lot, focusing on the concrete, the parked cars, anything but the images in her mind.

Like it or not, Sam was and would always be a part of Kyla's life and, consequently, of hers, and she was going to have to figure out a way to deal with him, as well as with any misplaced feelings she had about him.

She wished Sam and Kyla would hurry. Surely the emotional stress of being with her daughter would rescue her from the chaos of her own thoughts.

Finally, she saw them. Kyla walked toward the office wearing a white cotton top and floral-print skirt and looking frighteningly grown up.

When Marcie opened the door and stepped out, Kyla grinned and waved and Marcie's heart flip-flopped with pride. Her baby was so beautiful!

Sam followed close behind her. He wore a blue sport coat and gray slacks, and his hair was slightly mussed, in spite of obvious efforts to comb it into place.

The minute she saw him, her carefully thought-out, logical theories about the way her excitement at being with Kyla had spilled over onto her feelings for him dissolved and floated away on the summer wind.

Sam and Kyla both stirred a strong response in her, but the responses were not related, not even remotely similar.

And the scary part was, Sam's gaze on her burned with

an uneasy knowledge of the same inappropriate, surprised attraction.

"Hey, you look almost like an accountant today," Kyla exclaimed. "Kind of dressed up and official."

Marcie looked down at the severe lines of her suit. It was too conservative. She felt ill at ease and stuffy beside the easy casualness of her daughter and Sam.

"When I packed, this seemed generic enough for anything."

"It's cool." Kyla skipped backward as she talked, leading them toward the van. "Great color. Dad's always telling me I should wear blue to go with my eyes. You have blue eyes, too, so you should wear blue, too. Isn't that right, Dad?"

"Isn't what right?" Sam asked, in that special warm, teasing tone he used with Kyla. "That you have blue eyes, that Marcie has blue eyes, or that she should wear blue?"

Kyla groaned. "All of the above. Dad thinks you have great eyes, Marcie."

"I didn't say that!"

"But you do, don't you?" With a giggle, Kyla turned and darted the remaining few feet to the van, then climbed into the back.

Marcie stared at the pavement, embarrassed by Kyla's antics and uncertain how she should respond.

"You do," he said quietly, and for a fleeting instant, she thought he meant she had great eyes. "Have eyes like Kyla," he went on. "Or she has eyes like you, I guess. It's weird to see my daughter's eyes in a stranger's face."

How silly she'd been to think he would compliment her. She'd become involved in that make-believe world again.

They reached the van, and he opened the door for her. She made a futile effort not to appear clumsy as she negotiated the high step in her slim skirt.

Sam took her elbow, though the gesture did nothing at all to facilitate her climb and a lot to increase her clumsiness.

"Thank you," she said breathlessly as she sank into the seat.

"You're welcome." His voice was slightly husky, and he gazed at her for a fraction of a second too long before closing the door and going around to the driver's side.

Heaven help her, after years of feeling dead inside whenever a man touched her, she was suddenly, disastrously, attracted to the man who stood between her and her daughter.

Marcie entered the small church with Sam and Kyla. Sunlight, colored by the stained-glass windows, streamed in while an organist played softly. The sanctuary was half filled with people either waiting quietly or talking in hushed tones.

An older man standing at the rear of the church approached them.

"Good to see you again, Coach," he said, shaking Sam's hand. "Our boys going to win Conference this year?"

"Sure hope so. Summer workouts have been pretty promising."

The man turned to her with a smile. "I see you brought two beautiful women today, instead of just one. This must be—"

"Marcie Turner," Sam said, cutting the man off in midsentence. "A friend. Marcie, this is Wayne Cantrell."

The man handed them a printed schedule for the service, and they moved on.

Who had the man thought she was? A girlfriend? Did Sam have someone in his life?

He was single, attractive... Why shouldn't he?

Yet the idea of Sam with another woman called up unwelcome, painful, jealous feelings. She didn't want her daughter to have a stepmother. She didn't want Kyla to have to divide her loyalties between two mothers.

And, she realized with a shock of dismay, she didn't like the thought of another woman's filling the role she'd been playing, lifting her lips to Sam's kiss, feeling his hand on her arm as he helped her into the van.

Well, she could just get over that last absurdity. The chemistry between Sam and her wasn't going anywhere. It was merely an annoyance.

They settled into a pew midway down, Kyla on one side of her and Sam on the other.

Marcie tried to tune out her awareness of Sam sitting beside her, to relax and absorb the tranquillity all around her, be thankful that she was in church on Sunday morning with her daughter.

When they stood to sing, Marcie held the hymnal, and Sam leaned closer, one hand supporting the corner of the book, his shoulder pressing tantalizingly against hers. His scent of ballparks and summer mingled with soap and wrapped around her, invading her senses. His deep voice close to her ear sang the words of the familiar hymn in a slightly off-key, totally beguiling tone. From the corner of her eye, she could see his lips moving, and the memory of how those lips had felt on hers was far too vivid.

She didn't need this added complication in an already hopelessly complicated situation.

She sat through the service in a daze, her mind skittering in a thousand directions, trying to create order from this latest chaos. She didn't hear a word the preacher said, but she was preternaturally aware of every movement Sam made, of the way the fabric of his slacks outlined the muscles in his thighs when he crossed his legs, of the sprinkling of hairs on the back of his hands where they lay in his lap...of Sam.

When the service ended, Kyla burst from her seat. "Food, food, quick, before I pass out!" She lifted a hand to her forehead in a dramatic gesture as they stood to make their way to the door.

"You'll live," Sam replied dryly.

Marcie experienced a little light-headedness herself, with the combination of hunger and the way the force of the crowd pressed Sam's body against hers as they moved into the aisle.

Then they burst out into the warmth of the sun and the fresh air, leaving the artificial chill of the air-conditioned building. A blue jay shrieked triumphantly. Cicadas chirruped. The lilting song of a calliope danced on the summer breeze.

Kyla dashed away to talk to a group of girls her age, and Marcie was left alone with Sam...alone with him in spite of the people milling about, shaking hands, eyeing her speculatively and inviting her back to their church.

"Glad you could come today, Coach," an elderly woman said, tapping his chest with her rolled-up bulletin. "You don't come nearly often enough. Getting up early on Sunday is good for the soul. And this must be Kyla's aunt." She extended her hand to Marcie, who took it numbly. "Kyla's the spitting image of you. I never got to meet her mother, but it's clear Kyla didn't take after this big guy. Just visiting, are you? Well, it's awful nice to meet you."

Before Marcie could protest, the woman had sighted another friend and toddled off.

"That's what Wayne Cantrell was going to say when you interrupted him," she murmured, watching the woman point her out to someone else. "That's what everybody's wondering." She turned to Sam. His face was dark, his jaw set squarely. "What did Lisa look like?"

He took a deep breath. "She was short and brunette."

"So Kyla looks nothing like her."

"No."

"Or like you."

"No."

"Sam, we have to tell her the truth. This is a small town. You're a local celebrity. People are going to talk."

He smiled grimly. "They'll never even come close to figuring it out."

"But—"

Kyla darted in front of them, dancing backward toward the van, and Sam's and her discussion was ended. For the moment.

"Rachel's going to the carnival. Can I go, too?"

Her daughter's words sliced painfully through Marcie's heart. It was only normal that Kyla would rather go somewhere with a friend than with an adult she'd just met. Marcie knew that. But it still hurt.

"I thought you were going to have brunch with Marcie."

Don't, she wanted to say. As much as she yearned to be with her daughter, she didn't want it to be because Sam forced Kyla to do it.

"They have food at the carnival. Really neat food. You and Marcie can come with us."

"Kyla, we've already made plans."

Kyla turned to Marcie. "You wanta come with us?" Her expression was eager, as though she really would like Marcie to go.

Marcie thought of the restrictive clothing she wore, the dress shoes not meant for walking, the indigestible, greasy food the carnival would have. "You bet. Sounds like fun."

If her daughter wanted to trek across the Sahara desert in a ski suit, she'd go with her.

"We'll have to go change clothes first," Sam warned.

"All right! Come on, Rachel!" A dark-haired girl broke from the group and loped over to join them.

Sam looked around. "Your mother didn't come today, Rachel?"

"Nah. She said I could walk down to the carnival after church, and she'd pick me up later. I've got my shorts right here." She held aloft a canvas bag.

Sam shifted his gaze to Kyla. "So, did you kids plan to go by yourself?" he asked quietly.

"My mom said I could." Rachel looked slightly defiant.

"Kyla knows I don't like her going places by herself."

"Dad, we're both thirteen. Anyway, I asked you and Marcie to come with me, didn't I? And you said you would, so what's the problem?"

"We'll talk about this later, and you won't be thirteen for two weeks yet."

The reference to Sam speaking to Kyla later, presumably in private, at home, was a painful reminder that Marcie was not a part of her child's life. The mention of Kyla's approaching birthday lumped that pain into a large, hard ball just beneath her heart. Every year, that date had brought painful memories she had to work hard to repress.

Not this year, she promised herself. She only had two weeks, but somehow, by that day, she'd have a part in Kyla's life. Kyla's birthday this year would be an occasion to celebrate, not an occasion to lock herself in her condo, turn off the phone and wish the day over with as quickly as possible.

When everybody had changed to shorts and they were on the way to the carnival, Marcie listened to Kyla and

Rachel talking and giggling in the back seat of the van.

Then a note of seriousness crept into the young voices.

"If your dad marries that woman," Kyla said, "are you gonna have to call her *'Mother'?*"

"No way! She's not my mother. I'm gonna call her 'that woman' forever."

Marcie cringed as she eavesdropped on their conversation. Would there ever come a time when Kyla would want to call her *Mother?*

The girls were giggling again as Sam pulled into the roped-off parking area down the block from the church they'd attended earlier. "Corn dogs, cotton candy and the carousel, coming up!" he announced.

Kyla groaned. "Dad, we're practically teenagers. We're too old for the carousel!"

Sam glanced at Marcie as he pulled the keys from the ignition, and for a moment out of time they shared an *Our little girl's growing up* look. It was a good moment, a good beginning to their afternoon.

With unerring accuracy, Kyla and Rachel led them to the first food booth.

"Four corn dogs, lots of mustard," Sam ordered.

Clutching the messy concoctions, the four of them strolled among the rides and games. All around them, the carnies shouted, carousel music bubbled, and people wandered past, almost everybody greeting Sam.

"Can we ride the Tilt-a-Whirl first?" Kyla asked, still chewing her last bite.

"How about we do something a little tamer to start, like the Ferris wheel."

"The Ferris wheel?" Kyla complained. "*Boring.*"

"Yeah, Coach, we want to do the fun stuff," Rachel said.

"We have plenty of time to do it all," he assured them.

"Oh, well, the Ferris wheel will give you grown-ups a few minutes for your food to settle, so you won't barf on the Tilt-a-Whirl."

Sam grabbed her neck in the crook of his arm. "Don't be gross."

She giggled and pulled away, running ahead of them toward the line for the Ferris wheel. "Rachel and I get to sit above you two, just in case you toss your corn dogs."

Sam shook his head and smiled. "The things kids consider cool."

She nodded, watching Kyla lope away. A resurgence of jealousy of Sam's closeness and easy camaraderie with her daughter pierced her heart. At the same time, she felt overwhelming gratitude to him for his loving care of her child.

"Hurry!" Kyla called, beckoning them to the place she was saving in the line for the ride.

True to Kyla's pronouncement, she and Rachel got on first, then Sam and Marcie. The carny locked the bar, and Marcie found herself pressed more closely against Sam than in the church.

As the wheel began to turn, she looked back at Kyla and Rachel. Kyla grinned and waved, and then the girls started rocking their seat precariously.

"Be careful!" Marcie called.

"Relax. It's only a Ferris wheel, and they're practically teenagers. Just ask them. They'll tell you." Sam's teasing words were a slap in the face, once again reminding her that she had no place in her daughter's life.

But that would soon change. She was doing all she could to change it.

The wheel gained momentum, and as it spun around, she gave in to the sensation of weightlessness, of floating in space, instead of being firmly anchored in the metal seat...a euphoric, soaring feeling. She'd forgotten the exhilaration of being up so high, with the wind teasing at her hair…and beside her a ruggedly handsome football coach with broad shoulders and a tantalizing grin.

She felt young, a teenager again. She lifted her hair into the wind and turned to Sam with a reckless smile. "This is fun."

His answering smile lit a warmth deep inside her. "Yeah," he agreed. "It is."

So simple, yet it seemed such a long time since she'd had fun…since she'd dared to open up enough to have fun. In order to hide from the pain of losing her daughter, she'd burrowed away so deeply, she hadn't felt anything.

As they reached the top of the wheel's arc, Sam leaned forward over the safety bar. "What a view! We're on a hill here, so you can see just about the whole town."

"It's a nice town. Reminds me of the one where I grew up. The one I couldn't wait to leave."

Sam nodded as the wheel swung them down, replacing their view of trees and houses with the carnival grounds. "I guess everybody goes through that. Leave home to seek adventure in the big city."

"You didn't."

He turned to look at her, his eyes shining, more green than brown in the bright light. "Sure I did. This job was only the first step up the ladder. I fully expected to coach the Sooners one day. Maybe even get into pro ball."

"Why are you still here?"

"Because I want to be. I've had offers from bigger schools, even from a couple of small colleges, but I'm happy right here. I like the job, the people, the lifestyle, and it's a great place to raise a kid."

His words had the ring of complete honesty, and she

experienced a pang of wistful envy. Sam had everything she wanted, including her daughter's love.

"That must be wonderful, to be in command of your life, to do exactly what you want to do."

"You sound like you're not. You don't get to be an accountant by accident. You must have wanted it."

Marcie looked away from him as the wheel rose again. A breeze blew a strand of hair into her face, and she brushed it away. "I worked hard to get through college and grad school. It was what I wanted at the time. But I used to want to be a teacher, mold young intellects, all that idealistic stuff."

"So you changed your mind. I did, too. I wouldn't coach the Dallas Cowboys if they begged me to. What's wrong with changing your mind?"

"I don't know. Nothing, I guess. After Jenny died, I quit caring about all those lofty ideals. I suppose I was being selfish. I couldn't bear the thought of teaching some other mother's child, when mine was—when I thought mine was dead."

"Were you planning to teach accounting, then decided to do it instead of teaching?"

She shook her head. "No, I wanted to teach elementary school, preferably first or second grades. I never liked math until my freshman year at college. That time period was pretty much a blur at first. I didn't know what I wanted to do, but then I noticed that my math classes had become my favorite. Numbers were safe. Working with them took all my concentration and none of my emotions." She shivered, feeling suddenly naked and exposed. What was it about Sam that made her reveal parts of herself she kept carefully hidden from everybody else? "Now that I've found Kyla, everything seems different," she concluded.

"Why should it be different?" he asked defensively. "If

you were happy with your job before— Were you happy with it?''

"I guess. I never thought about it.''

"So why are you thinking now? How did finding Kyla change everything in your life?''

She faced him directly. "Because if my mother hadn't lied to me, my life would have been entirely different. Everything would have been different.''

"Not necessarily better.''

The ride ended, and they stepped onto solid ground, their respective roles in this drama again clear.

Marcie moved a couple of feet away from Sam. The motion of the Ferris wheel had lifted her up, off the earth, out of the muddled reality of her world, and she, who never talked to anyone about her personal life, had been uncharacteristically open with Sam.

Of all people, why had she felt compelled to talk to him? He was the one person she didn't dare allow access to her secrets, her doubts and fears, and the power that came with knowing them.

Kyla and Rachel charged out of their seat, and she resolutely put her concerns aside.

In a wild frenzy, the girls ran from one ride to another, apparently determined to experience everything the small carnival had to offer.

Rachel's mother arrived shortly after four o'clock to take her daughter home, but Kyla showed no signs of slowing down.

"Candy apples!'' she exclaimed, charging up to another booth.

Marcie groaned. "More food?''

"*Teenager* is another word for *eating machine*,'' Sam said.

"Okay, you two, pay attention," Kyla said. "This is important. Candy or caramel?"

"Candy," Sam declared. "Who wants to get that messy, sticky stuff all over them? Yuck!"

Kyla put her fists on her narrow hips. "Just ignore him, Marcie. He's only saying that because he knows I love caramel."

"Me too," Marcie agreed. "I like caramel best, too." Was a taste for caramel apples hereditary? she wondered giddily.

Shaking his head in mock consternation, Sam stepped up to the booth to get the apples.

"Dad's pretty cool, isn't he?" Kyla said. "You like him, don't you?"

Marcie considered the question. Did she like him? She was attracted to him, drawn to him in a compelling, elemental way. His touch, his kiss, his gaze on her, all set her on fire. But did she like him?

She knew she didn't dare let herself get involved in any sort of emotional entanglement with him. This was far too important. She had to stay objective.

Kyla giggled. "You're blu-u-ushing," she sang. "It's okay if you like my dad. He likes you, too. I know these things."

Sam strode over with the apples, putting a welcome end to the conversation.

But Marcie's thoughts didn't end. She didn't like the idea of Kyla believing she and Sam were involved, and her uneasiness about the situation had just increased exponentially with Kyla's teasing remarks. It would be disorienting enough for her to learn Marcie's true identity; she shouldn't have to adjust to the fact that Sam's and Marcie's relationship had been a lie, too.

One more reason to tell her the truth soon.

"Look! A baseball game," Kyla said. "Win me that big purple dinosaur, Dad!"

"You've got a room full of stuffed animals," Sam protested, but he looked pleased as he sauntered over, picked up a baseball and knocked all the pins down three times in a row to claim the requested prize.

Kyla cheered and applauded, and Marcie joined her.

"Okay," Sam said, refusing to relinquish Kyla's dinosaur to her. "Your turn. I'll hold this guy while you win his brother."

"Aw, Dad, you know I'm not as good as you are."

"Only because you're not as old as I am. Give it your best shot."

She wasn't as good as Sam, but she was good enough to win one of the smaller animals. Marcie and Sam cheered and applauded, and in keeping with her crazy mood swings of the past couple of days, her totally ambivalent feelings, Marcie felt a bond with Sam—a bond of pride in their daughter.

"Okay, Marcie. You choose what color. This one's yours."

"The little purple one who looks just like yours."

Kyla claimed the toy, then turned to Marcie, holding it at arm's length, grinning mischievously. "Your turn. I'll hold him while you win one for Dad. Maybe even another big one. You ever been on a major-league baseball team?"

Marcie laughed. "Not even a neighborhood baseball team. You obviously have Mitch's athletic ability."

From behind her, Marcie heard Sam's quick intake of breath. Shocked horror brought hot blood rushing to flame her cheeks as she realized what she'd said.

Kyla looked at her curiously. "Who's Mitch?"

"Oh, uh, someone I knew a long time ago. I meant to say, you have your father's athletic ability," she stammered, trying to cover up her lapse, but unwilling to name Sam as Kyla's father.

She darted forward and picked up the ball, anxious to leave the dangerous territory she'd blundered into. "Okay, let's see how badly I can do this."

"No, no," Kyla protested. "Not like that, not with your whole hand. Hold it between your first two fingers and your thumb. Like this. Fingers on the top. That's good. Now don't aim. Just look at the pins, and your hand will do the rest."

With her lack of expertise and her distress over her slip about Mitch, Marcie was surprised that she actually knocked over one pin.

"Not bad," Kyla enthused. "This time, step back to about here. Plant your right foot, and as you start to throw lean forward on your left. When your left foot hits the ground, release the ball."

Sam stood looking on as his daughter coached Marcie, repeating the instructions and techniques he'd taught her. He had to admit, it was a touching scene. Mother and daughter, with the daughter doing the educating. And Marcie was eating it up. Her face glowed like a two-hundred-watt bulb.

She'd been doing a lot of glowing today. She was having a good time, and so was he. In fact, for a while, he'd forgotten the dynamics of this triangle. He'd given in to the seductive closeness of her slim body, her soft, womanly scent, the memory of their far-too-brief kiss, the intimacy of their talk on the Ferris wheel...the dizzying exhilaration of teetering on the brink of a new relationship.

But the new relationship wasn't between Marcie and him. Everything she said and did today had been in the interest of reaching her daughter. Even her slip about Kyla's inherited abilities was one more step in that direction. He was sure she hadn't done it intentionally. It was just that all her efforts, conscious and unconscious, were geared toward that goal.

She was attracted to him. He'd seen it in the startled, embarrassed, smoky-eyed way she looked whenever he touched her, in the way her lips clung to his last night. But that attraction was secondary to her need to regain her daughter—his daughter.

He could understand that. She was, first and foremost, a mother, the way nature had intended. Lisa had found that instinct even with a child she hadn't carried inside her body.

He'd lost Lisa twice, once to her need to mother and once to death. He wasn't going to lose Kyla to Marcie, and he wasn't going to lose his common sense to Marcie's electric touches, to her slim legs emerging from her khaki shorts, to her smooth cheeks that flushed so becomingly pink beneath eyes the same shade of blue as the morning glories that had grown up the side of the house when he was a boy...

Kyla's giggles broke into his thoughts.

"I'm afraid we have to face reality," Marcie said ruefully. "I'll never be a baseball player."

"Dad always said you should never give up. But..." Kyla giggled again. "I think it's a good thing you took up accounting instead of sports. Let's go find some ice cream. I need a sugar fix after that workout."

Kyla handed Marcie the small dinosaur she'd won for her, and they both turned to look at him.

Two pairs of blue eyes, so similar, yet so different. He'd lost his heart to the one pair without a single regret. However, unless he kept a closer guard against that second pair, he could see nothing but trouble ahead.

"It's time to go." Sam's words came out more brusquely

than he'd intended, bringing a stunned expression to Kyla's face and a shuttered, distant expression to Marcie's.

Well, it couldn't be helped. He was feeling brusque. Not to mention frightened and spinning helplessly in the middle of a black, raging tornado that was turning his home, his life and his heart inside out.

Chapter Seven

"Are you coming back next weekend, Marcie?" Kyla asked that evening as Sam pulled up next to her car in the almost deserted Holiday Inn parking lot. "Have you asked her to go out with us again, Dad?"

With us. His daughter was completely taken with Marcie.

He looked at Kyla's beaming, expectant face, then at the same expression on Marcie's.

"Gee, Princess, do you think you'll ever outgrow this shyness?" he asked.

"Probably not. What do you say? We could do Robber's Cave State Park, or go bowling, or—"

"Isn't this the weekend you're supposed to go see Grandmother and Granddad Kramer?"

Kyla made a face, and he felt a shiver run down his spine. Over the past few years, she'd begun to complain good-naturedly about leaving her friends and activities to visit either set of grandparents. It had never bothered him before. It was just part of growing up, becoming a teenager, moving out of the family circle into the rest of the world.

Now, suddenly, he saw her reluctance as a threat. She'd taken immediately to Marcie and wanted to spend time with her, rather than with Lisa's parents. Was he just being paranoid, or had she sensed on an instinctual level that a blood connection existed?

He wanted to pull her close, hold on to her for dear life.

He settled for reaching back and yanking her ponytail as she leaned forward between the seats.

"Lisa's parents have a cabin at Lake Eufala, about fifteen minutes from here," he explained. "When Lisa died, they bought this cabin just to be close to their ungrateful granddaughter."

"They're *bor*ing."

"We define *boring* as when they make her behave instead of letting her run around like a wild heathen. They love her very much. She's their only grandchild. Lisa was their only child." Surely Marcie could understand what losing a child meant. "No matter what happens, Kyla will always be their granddaughter."

Marcie's eyes widened, and he realized his voice had risen threateningly.

"Of course they will." Kyla twisted around to give him a curious glance. "You can't divorce your grandparents, silly. Or your kids."

"Are you sure about that last?"

"Yep."

"In that case, I'm stuck with you. And I'm going to make sure you go to see your grandparents next weekend."

Kyla groaned, but then a sly grin spread over her face as she looked from him to Marcie and back again. "Truth, Dad. Are you sending me away so you can spend the weekend alone with Marcie?"

"No!" he and Marcie exclaimed at the same time.

"Where do you come up with this stuff?" Sam demanded. "No, don't tell me. I don't think I want to know."

Kyla rolled her eyes. "Dad, I'm nearly thirteen. Hey, is Marcie coming to my birthday party weekend after next? My birthday's on Thursday, but no matter when it comes, we always have a party that weekend, because it's the last weekend before school starts," she explained to Marcie. "Kind of like a good-news-bad-news party."

Sam stared straight ahead, out the windshield of the van. Part of him wanted to refuse. Lisa's parents would be there. Thank goodness his parents had other plans and couldn't fly up from Florida for the occasion. But Kyla's friends would be there. His friends would be there.

And everyone would be speculating as to Marcie's status in his life.

The inevitable was rapidly approaching.

But even if he could have prevented her coming, he wouldn't have had the heart to. Especially on Kyla's birthday, on the day Marcie had given birth to and lost her baby, she should be with her.

"Of course Marcie can come," he said. "If she wants to."

"Thank you," Marcie said, her voice soft and golden as the fading summer sunlight. "I'd love to come. What would you like for a birthday present, Kyla?"

"Oh, you can't bring a present. That's one of Dad's rules. Only family can bring gifts. He says I have to appreciate friendship as a gift from everybody else."

Even though he didn't dare look at her, Sam could feel the tension and pain emanating from Marcie at Kyla's announcement.

"That's a wonderful sentiment," Marcie said, breaking the brittle silence. "I certainly approve of the concept. But suppose someone really wants to bring you something? What do you do then?''

She was ostensibly asking Kyla, but Sam knew the question—the challenge—was directed toward him. He wiped the perspiration from his upper lip. "Since I made the rule, I can make the exceptions," he said, trying to sound as though it were his idea, "and I say we allow Marcie to be the exception. She can bring you a gift, if it isn't very expensive."

"Guess that lets out a big-screen TV."

"Guess it does."

"Oh, well! So, Marcie, you won't have to take out a loan to come to my party. It's Saturday after next, six o'clock, our place. We'll have burgers again and hot dogs. That's all Dad knows how to cook. And Grandmother Kramer always brings a big cake with lots of flowers and stuff on it. She makes pretty cakes, but they don't taste as good as yours."

Marcie smiled. "Thank you for the compliment, and for inviting me. I'll be there." She spoke to Kyla, but her eyes were on Sam, full of gratitude, and for a fleeting instant he resented the fact that she was grateful for the chance to see Kyla again, not the chance to see him.

He shoved that stupid feeling aside. "We'll look forward to it."

"Me too." She smiled, then looked down at her hands, clutching her purse in her lap. "Well. I really enjoyed the weekend. Thanks for having me over and for letting me come to the carnival with you."

She reached for the door handle.

"Hang on, I'll get that," Sam protested, opening his own.

"I can do it."

He ignored her, loped around the van and opened her

door. He'd show her that manners still prevailed in small towns.

But as she stepped down, taking his hand for support, her body so close to his that he fancied he could feel the electrical impulses of life coming from her, he realized politeness hadn't been his motive at all.

He continued to hold her hand, and she made no effort to withdraw it. She gazed at him, uncertainty and desire warring on her guileless face. The afternoon sun nestled in her hair, and her eyes perfectly mirrored the Oklahoma sky.

"I'm reading a book, Dad!" Kyla called. "I'm not looking at anything except the page in front of me!"

Marcie's full lips, and the corners of her eyes, tilted upward. "She doesn't have a book in the van, does she?"

Sam chuckled. "No. And even if she did, she wouldn't be looking at it. She expects...uh..."

Damn! He could feel hot blood rushing to his face. He was blushing and tongue-tied, as if he were a teenager on his first date.

Of course, this was only a pretend date.

And his daughter expected him to do more than *pretend* to kiss Marcie good-night.

Marcie's lips parted infinitesimally, the movement so slight that he wouldn't have noticed if he wasn't watching so closely, if his whole world hadn't been suddenly centered on those lips.

He lifted his hands to her shoulders, needing to touch her, to hold her against him and knowing this wasn't the time or the place or even the lifetime. She spread her hands on his chest, slid them around him, holding on to his back, and he could have sworn he felt the separate imprint of each of her fingers where they touched him, ten slender columns of fire on his back.

He lowered his mouth to hers, moving in slow motion,

driving himself crazy with the enforced wait, the need to kiss her in conflict with the need to savor every tantalizing sensation along the way, with the knowledge that the kiss had to be brief and perfunctory and unsatisfying.

When his lips finally touched hers, all *knowledge* disappeared, drowned in the magic of the way her mouth moved on his, the lingering taste of corn dogs and caramel apples, the fantasy day they'd spent together.

Somewhere in the back of his brain, a voice shouted at him that he should stop kissing Marcie, that he'd performed quite adequately to convince Kyla, and what was he trying to convince Kyla of, anyway?

But he wasn't listening to that voice. It wasn't shouting nearly loud enough to drown out the sound of his own blood rushing past his ears, of Marcie's heart beating against his, of the music of her kisses.

It was Marcie who pulled away, giving him a fleeting look of desire, confusion and fear before she whirled around and began fumbling with the lock on her car door.

Sam drew in a shaky breath, plowed trembling fingers through his hair and walked slowly away, back to his van. His heart was racing, the blood pounding through his veins, his breathing hard and fast.

Who the hell was he kidding? That kiss hadn't been for Kyla's benefit. In fact, if Kyla hadn't been around, if they hadn't been in the middle of a public parking lot... No, he didn't dare think about that, not if he had any thoughts of getting back in the van and having a reasonable conversation with his daughter.

Kyla was climbing into the front seat as he got in. "She likes you, Dad." The delight in her voice was obvious. "This sounds pretty serious, letting her bring me a family gift."

Serious? You could say that, he thought. *My-whole-*

world-at-stake serious. "I barely know her. It's a little early to be talking serious." He deliberately ignored the implications of permitting Marcie to bring Kyla a birthday present.

Kyla rolled down her window and stuck her head out. "Bye, Marcie! See you at my party!"

"Goodbye, Kyla! I can't wait."

Sam leaned around, needing to see whether that kiss had left her as disturbed as it had him, but her attention and wide smile were focused solely on Kyla.

She'd responded when he kissed her. He knew that. But the kiss hadn't meant to her what it meant to him. Immediately her attention had returned to Kyla, to her child.

He twisted the key in the ignition and stomped on the gas. The engine roared to life with a ferocity that startled him, and prompted Kyla to sit back in her seat.

From the corner of his eye, he saw Marcie's car moving across the lot toward the highway.

"I don't think you should worry too much about that Mitch guy. By the time people get as old as you and Marcie, they've nearly always had somebody in their past."

"Thanks for the benefit of your experience, O wise one," he returned, but his heart wasn't in the flippant response. He was plenty worried about *that Mitch guy,* but not in the way Kyla thought.

Following Marcie's small car, he guided the van onto the highway, heading in the opposite direction from the one she took. After he pulled out, he looked in his rearview mirror, but the road curved, and already she was gone. All he saw was the empty highway and the sun glowing brightly on the horizon, the last blaze of glory before it disappeared into the night.

He returned his gaze to the road ahead.

"This is the first woman I've...uh...dated that you seem to get along with."

"Yeah."

"I always assumed you resented them because you thought they were trying to take your mother's place."

"Nah. They were just dorky. They all acted so dumb, especially trying to suck up to me when they really didn't like me. They just do it so you'll like them better."

"Marcie—in your vernacular—sucks up to you. Sometimes I think maybe she's trying a little too hard to win you over. So why is she different?"

Kyla cocked her head to one side as she considered that for a minute. "Yeah, she does try too hard sometimes. But I don't think it's just because of you. I think she really likes me. Don't you?"

"Yes," he admitted. "I do." Kyla was amazingly perceptive. Even she'd noticed that Marcie was interested in her, not him.

She nodded. "That's why she's different." She was silent for a moment, and when she finally spoke, her voice was unaccustomedly quiet. "Mom loved me a lot, didn't she?"

"Oh, yes, sweetheart. She loved you more than anything. Her last words were about you."

"I remember when she used to take me to the park and then we'd go for ice cream, and at night she'd sing to me and read me stories, and once she got me a blue dress and I fell and tore it but she didn't get mad. I don't remember very much, though, so sometimes I concentrate really hard on what I do remember, so I won't ever forget it."

"You were barely five years old when she died. You couldn't possibly remember much. It's okay not to."

"Do you think she remembers me? Do you think she still loves me?"

Sam wished they weren't on the highway. This was one of those times when his daughter needed to be held and cuddled and reassured. "Of course she does. Your—" Thinking of Marcie, he hesitated before using the word *mother*. But Lisa had been Kyla's mother, whether or not she'd given birth to her. "Your mother's watching over you from up in heaven, and she loves you even more than when she was down here with you."

"Rachel's mom hates her dad's new girlfriend. She doesn't want Rachel to have anything to do with her. Rachel hates her, too."

Suddenly he realized where this conversation had come from.

He stole a quick glance at her soft, childish features, golden from the dying sun, creased with concern, surrounded by wispy tendrils of blond hair escaping from her ponytail. For his daughter's peace of mind, he was going to have to sell himself down the river, plead Marcie's case.

"Your mom and I didn't get a divorce. Your mom died, and because she loves you so much, she wants you to be happy. She—" He swallowed hard, unsure whether he could say the words he knew he had to say. "If I were to, say, get married again or something, and you cared about that woman and wanted her to be your, um, stepmother, your mother would understand. She'd want that."

From the corner of his eye, he could see her nod, but he couldn't tell whether she was convinced or not. Anyway, he hadn't addressed the real issue. This wasn't about her accepting a new wife of his. This was about her real mother appearing out of nowhere to disrupt their lives and set Kyla to worrying about being disloyal to Lisa.

The last ray of light from the sun disappeared as they went down a hill, and twilight engulfed them.

The shadows outside loomed, broken by the glaring neon

lights of businesses along the highway. The bright colors glowed with promises they couldn't fulfill. Inside were the same service stations, restaurants, motels and convenience stores that looked so mundane in the light of day.

The carnival they'd gone to earlier was like that, all dazzling and happy on the outside, but really only truckloads of mechanical parts erected on a dusty field. For a little while, in that false atmosphere, he and Marcie had seemed to be something they weren't. Every step she took in the direction of reclaiming her place as Kyla's mother was a step away from the pretense of anything between her and him.

But where did that mind-numbing kiss fit into all the pretenses?

The feel of her lips on his, the tumult she stirred in him, were very real.

And didn't mean a damn thing. Not to her, not in the overall scheme of things. Not when balanced against her need to have her daughter.

He flipped on his blinker and turned down a side street, heading for the comfort and safety of home, a place that glowed with the genuine light of love, of Kyla.

He had no idea what was going to happen to that light.

Marcie stared into the darkness ahead of her. The hour-and-a-half trip home seemed to be taking forever, and occasionally she had to check to be sure she hadn't taken a wrong turn.

Jumbled thoughts darted in and out of her consciousness, leaving her thoroughly confused...happy one moment and despairing the next.

Right on the heels of the momentous thrill of being invited to her daughter's birthday party had come the realization that the evening was over. She hadn't wanted it to be over. She hadn't wanted to leave Kyla.

Or Sam.

She lifted the fingers of one hand to her treacherous mouth, which had betrayed her with its yearning for Sam's lips, with its eager response to him.

She'd thought about the possibility of kissing Sam when she realized it was time to leave. She'd grabbed for the van door and tried to escape because she wanted him to kiss her. She'd wanted it all day, every time he looked at her, touched her, spoke to her. She'd wanted it ever since that first tentative kiss in the street in front of his house, and probably before that, in between bouts of anxiety over getting to know her daughter.

Then, tonight, he'd helped her down from the van and she'd stood so close to him that she could see the golden striations in his hazel eyes, smell the carefree scents of the carnival mixed with his own compelling masculine scents.

There was something in Sam that drew her, against all reason and logic. He was dangerous, and not just in a physical way. She was finding it far too easy to relax around him, to talk to him about things she'd never discussed with anyone...and to seek his touch and let herself get lost in the resulting tidal wave.

She had to control those misguided yearnings. She'd been given a second chance with her daughter, with her life, and she couldn't afford to blow it.

As she drove away, she'd stared back at the blue van in her rearview mirror, and the need to be inside that van, going home with Kyla and Sam, burned inside her chest with a white-hot flame.

But not the way she'd been—an outsider fumbling for a place, for acceptance. She wanted to be a part of the easy, comfortable, loving relationship Sam and Kyla shared.

And she had to face the painful truth. That fantasy wasn't possible.

Sam had thirteen years of day-to-day living with Kyla, and no matter what she did now, that was something Marcie would never have. One of the first times they spoke, Sam had asked her where she thought she'd fit into his relationship with Kyla. She hadn't known then, and she still didn't know, even after spending the weekend with her.

It was, she thought, ironic that she'd felt dating Mitch Randall would help her fit into the in crowd in high school. It hadn't, of course.

However she'd gone on to succeed in college and in her career.

Now, thirteen years later, she again felt on the outside looking in.

But she wasn't eighteen anymore. Somewhere there had to be a niche where she could fit into Kyla's life, and until she found it, she couldn't give up or let herself get side-tracked by Sam's laughing eyes or the intoxicating, mind-numbing effect he had on her senses whenever he touched her.

When she walked in the door of her condo, her phone was ringing. It was probably her mother, and the phone had probably been ringing every ten minutes for the past couple of hours, maybe even continuously. She considered letting the answering machine pick up, but knew her mother would call all night until she got to talk to her.

She set her bag on the floor and went over to the break-fast bar to answer the call.

"Hi, sweetheart. I'm so glad you're finally home. I was getting worried."

"I told you I didn't know when I'd be back."

"Well, tell me all about my granddaughter." Anne Turner's voice was filled with anticipation, as if she were any grandmother, as if she hadn't been the one to give her granddaughter away to strangers.

"She's wonderful. Beautiful, brilliant, talented. I couldn't have asked for a more perfect daughter."

"I want to hear everything!"

Marcie hadn't been able to forgive her mother, and didn't really want to share the miracle of Kyla with her. Yet, as she began to tell about the events of her meetings with Kyla, she found herself bubbling over, eager to have someone to talk to who'd be as excited as she, as thrilled to know that Kyla was an honor student, that Kyla was the star pitcher of her softball team…every minute detail that anyone else would find meaningless, anyone but a mother or a grandmother.

Or a father.

But she couldn't share her delight with Sam.

Nor did she tell her mother about the good-night kisses, or the way Sam made her feel.

"Do you think it would be all right if I came to her birthday party with you?" Anne's voice was unusually tentative.

"I don't know. I'll ask Sam." As she spoke the words, resentment nagged at Marcie. She didn't really want her mother to come, but at the same time, she didn't like having to ask permission for her mother to attend her daughter's birthday party.

Nevertheless, she did have to. It was Sam's party, at Sam's house, and Sam had control of her daughter.

"I'll ask," she repeated. "I'm sure it'll be fine."

She wasn't at all sure. Nor was she sure whether Kyla's third grandmother would be allowed to bring a gift, *like family.*

"I wish we didn't have to wait two weeks," her mother went on, her attitude returning to normal. "Those people

aren't really her grandparents. I don't see why they shoul
get to see her instead of us.''

Sharing her daughter with her mother had been a warm
satisfying experience, but Anne's attitude jerked her bac
to reality, to the reason they had to wait two weeks, th
reason she had to ask permission for Kyla's grandmothe
to attend her birthday party, the reason Sam was in contro
of Marcie's life.

''Because you gave her to them,'' she said, keeping he
voice quiet, not allowing her pointless anger to show.

Her mother was silent for a moment. When she spoke
her tone was indignant. ''Really, Marcie, you've got t
learn to put the past behind you. This obsessing abou
what's over and done will only upset you.''

Suppressed anger boiled in Marcie's gut. What he
mother said was right, but coming from her, with no tain
of guilt or remorse, the sentiment left a bitter taste.

''I'm very tired. I'm going to bed now. Good night
mother.''

Another confrontation would serve no purpose except t
add to her own distress.

That night, as she lay in bed, Marcie found hersel
strangely restless.

Tomorrow the alarm would go off at six, as it alway
did, and she'd go to work and then come home again, a
she always did. She'd confessed to Sam that being an ac
countant hadn't been her first choice of a career, but sh
didn't dislike her job. It was challenging enough to hol
her interest, and the income provided a comfortable life fo
herself and for her mother.

Tonight, for the first time, she felt a vague, elusive dis
content.

She'd carefully walled herself off in one safe corne
working with numbers and not people, keeping her socia

contacts at arm's length, never getting emotionally involved with anyone.

Then Kyla had burst onto the scene, brimming with life and vitality. She had been given another chance with her daughter.

It was incredible and wonderful but it was scary.

And along with Kyla came Sam. Sam, with hazel eyes surrounded by sunbursts, big hands that made her own hands feel fragile when he held them, a smile that seemed to come straight from his heart and go straight to hers and lips that stirred unexplored fires inside her innermost being.

Her whole life was changing, turning upside down…for the second time.

Suddenly that corner wasn't safe anymore.

So easily, so quickly, her life had plummeted down the wrong road thirteen years ago. Just as easily, it could take the wrong turn again, if she didn't get everything exactly right.

She recalled her earlier thought that Sam was dangerous.

That wasn't true. It was only her reaction to him that was dangerous, that desire he evoked, that yearning to turn loose, to relax her vigilance, to let herself get caught up in the strong emotions he unleashed in her…to give him power in her life.

Sam was a good person, a good father to Kyla, but his goal was in direct opposition to hers.

Her mother was a good person and a good mother, and in achieving her goal, she'd stolen Marcie's dreams.

If she had any chance to make things come out right this time, she had to stay aloof and detached from Sam, allow him no control, take charge of circumstances herself.

She couldn't avoid him. He was a part of Kyla's life.

She had to associate with him, talk to him, spend time with him, work things out with him.

But while she reached for her daughter with one hand she needed to hold on tightly with the other to that safe corner. Her future and Kyla's depended on it.

Chapter Eight

Saturday afternoon, Sam pulled into the main entrance of the small cemetery in Hillsdale. He'd phoned Marcie that morning to ask the exact location of Jenny's grave, wanting to visit there while Kyla was out of town.

Rather than give him directions, however, Marcie had wanted to take him, and he'd agreed. He understood; he didn't want her to visit Kyla alone.

Marcie was waiting just inside the main entrance. He followed her car through several turns, until she parked in a spot indistinguishable to him from anywhere else they'd passed. It was a good thing she'd met him.

He climbed down from the van. Marcie stood beside the path, holding a bouquet of daisies.

Without a word, she turned and led him past several markers toward a huge oak tree.

The gauzy yellow dress she wore floated about her legs, and her golden hair swayed with the graceful motion of her walk. In the deep silence, broken only by the rasp of grasshoppers and an outburst from a cicada, she almost seemed to be a spirit herself, guiding him to the small grave.

She knelt and put the flowers in a permanent vase affixed to the side of the stone.

He hesitated, feeling a little like an intruder.

Did she feel that way about entering his and Kyla's lives? Aware she was intruding, but unable to stop herself?

"I've loved her for so long," Marcie said quietly, "it doesn't seem right to give her up. I'll miss her."

Sam didn't know what to say. He knelt beside her and traced the carved letters with his finger.

Jennifer Nicole Turner

"I know," he finally said. He did know. He couldn't give up Kyla, either.

"I brought pictures of her. I only have these two, but we could have copies made."

He looked up, his heart wrenching with the generosity of the gift Marcie was offering him. Tears glistened on her eyelashes as she handed him the photographs.

"Thank you" was all he could say.

He recognized the baby immediately from the brief glimpse he'd had of her before Dr. Franklin whisked her away to try to save her life. She was pale, ashen, lacking the healthy red color of a newborn, of Kyla when she'd been placed in his arms the next day.

He cleared his throat, trying to get rid of the lump that had formed there. "Jennifer," he said, testing the name. "Jenny. It doesn't seem right that Lisa and I weren't there to bury her, or that we never visited her grave."

"I was there," Marcie reminded him, her soft voice blending into the summer afternoon. "I took care of her the way you took care of my baby."

"I know you did. It's just that—" He shook his head. "This is all so strange. I loved this little girl. I know I only saw her once for a few seconds, but I loved her for nine months. Lisa used to put my hand on her stomach, and I'd feel her kick. Before she was even born, I'd have given my life for her." He felt the tears on his own cheeks.

"I know," Marcie whispered, and suddenly he knew, too. From his heart, he understood her need to have Kyla back.

Without thinking, he wrapped her in his arms, holding her close, sharing their grief, so different, yet so much the same. She leaned against him, taking and offering comfort, and peace stole over him, a peace he hadn't known since this nightmare began…actually, since Lisa died.

Touching Marcie, holding her, seemed to create a bond, a connection, with the two of them, Jenny, Kyla and Lisa, the intertwined fates finally coming together.

"She was so tiny," Marcie said. "I've always worried about her being out there all alone. Oh, I know God's with her, but a baby needs her mother. I feel better knowing Lisa's there to take care of her."

"I never thought of it that way. When Lisa died, the hardest thing for her was leaving her daughter. She loved Kyla so much. But she never even got to hold Jenny in her arms. Now she can."

For a few moments, they held each other in silence. Marcie's body against his felt so natural and right. He never wanted to let her go, never wanted to relinquish this feeling of tranquillity, of the world untangling.

"I'd like to bring Kyla here after we explain everything to her," Marcie said. "I know you'll think this is crazy, but I feel as if they're sisters, as if they're both my babies."

For the first time, he didn't pull away from the idea of telling Kyla. "I know," he murmured into her hair. Somehow, as he sat beside Jenny's grave with Marcie in his arms, surrounded by the hot scent of dusty summer, embraced by the cool shade of the oak tree, with the sun dappling bright spots around them, it seemed normal and non-threatening that he should tell Kyla the truth.

A squirrel darted past them and up the tree.

"Oh!" Marcie jumped, echoing his own surprise at the intrusion of the outside world. She stood, brushing grass from her dress, avoiding his gaze, as if she felt uncomfortable with the unaccustomed closeness they'd just shared. "It's getting late. I guess I'd better go."

"Yeah, me too." As though coming out of a trance, he felt awkward and ill at ease.

Wordlessly they crossed the cemetery to their cars.

Sam started to open Marcie's door for her, then realized he still held the pictures of Jenny. With one last look, he handed them to her. "Thanks for letting me see those. I really would appreciate it if you'd have copies made."

"I will." Her gaze lingered on his face, and he wondered if she, too, was searching for that brief connection they'd shared, then lost.

He nodded, and she slid into her car. He closed the door behind her, strangely reluctant to let her go.

She started the engine, then rolled down her window. "Do you know how to get out of here, or do you want to follow me back?"

He leaned on the open window, his face level with hers. "I can find my way."

"I'll get the pictures to you in a few days."

"Good. Thanks." He stepped back from the car, then leaned down again. "Would you like to see pictures of Kyla?"

Her smile was radiant, her delight obvious, kindling a warm glow inside his chest.

He was in his van on the road to McAlester with Marcie following behind before the full impact of her happiness hit him. Marcie wasn't coming to his house to see him. She was coming to see pictures of his daughter…their daughter.

He'd somehow let himself get carried away with her nearness, with the peculiar connection that existed between them, their two mutual daughters. Grieving together for a dead child they both loved had united them in a way most people were never united.

He understood that, but he'd let everything get tangled up in the feelings between the two of them, and that was all wrong. Whatever existed between Marcie and him was only there by dint of reflecting off Kyla and Jenny.

The only reason she was coming to his house was to look at pictures of Kyla.

Wasn't that what he'd invited her to do?

So why the heck did he resent it?

Dumb question. He knew why.

Because Marcie had the ability to turn him inside out, to tug on his heart one minute and his libido the next. Because one minute they shared the love of two daughters, a bond he had with nobody else on earth, and the next he wanted her the way a man wants a woman. It was a lethal combination.

Bad enough that this woman wanted to take his daughter. He damn sure didn't need to let himself get so turned around and confused he couldn't see straight enough to defend Kyla…to defend himself.

Marcie pulled up in front of Sam's house and got out of her car. As she walked down the sidewalk, she watched Sam jump from his van, open the door to the old detached garage, put the vehicle inside, then come back out. A lot of extra steps, compared to pulling into her underground parking garage, then getting into an elevator and going up to her condo.

But her condo never greeted her with the homey, warm feeling that Sam's house exuded.

She couldn't have picked a better father for her daughter, she thought as he stepped up beside her on the porch and stooped to unlock the front door.

"I'd apologize for the house not being very clean, but it's always this way. Last weekend was about the best it ever gets."

"We can look at Kyla's pictures just as easily in a messy house as a clean one," she reassured him. What she didn't say was that her condo was always immaculate...and empty of the warmth of Sam's old, messy home, with its time-wasting detached garage.

He opened the door, and she moved past him into the cool, dim interior of the house. He followed her in, his shoulder brushing hers, the casual, accidental touch vibrating through her body. She heard a sharp intake of breath, but couldn't tell if it was from him or her. Maybe both.

He looked down at her, his gaze devouring her, reflecting the same chaotic attraction she felt.

Dismay mingled with desire as she was forced to admit to herself that all her resolutions of the night before had vaporized in the heat of the August day. She'd been disarmed by the warmth of Sam's body as he held her in the cemetery. Now his nearness brought a bolt of heat lightning as they stood so close, alone in his house, with Kyla out of town and the solitude of night approaching.

She whirled away and started across the room, moving with no purpose in mind except to get away from Sam, from her own treacherous yearnings.

At the cemetery, she'd been comfortable with him, all her emotions natural and acceptable. But at the cemetery they'd shared a common grief. Away from that all-encompassing emotion, the rest of the world came back, including their strained, confusing relationship, her need to avoid debilitating involvement with him.

On a small table, she spotted a framed picture of a girl's softball team. Grateful for an excuse for her flight, as well as for something to focus on, to draw her attention from Sam, she snatched up the photograph.

Kyla, holding aloft a softball and beaming, stood beside Sam in the second row.

"The Gremlins." Sam's voice came from somewhere behind her. "Appropriately named." Though his words were light, his voice sounded stiff—or maybe it only came to her ears that way, filtered through her own stiff, uncomfortable awareness.

"Is this Rachel in the front row?"

"Number seventeen? That's her."

"She looks different. Younger. Happier."

"She was a year younger in that picture. They change fast at that age. That was also before her parents' divorce. So I guess she was happier."

"That's too bad. It seems to have hit her really hard."

"It hasn't been easy for her. Divorce always hurts the kids the most. It doesn't help that her dad's trying to force his new girlfriend on her."

Marcie turned to look at Sam, her heart clenching painfully. Was he drawing a parallel between the trauma of Rachel's having a surrogate mother forced on her and the potential trauma of Kyla's having a real mother forced on her?

"Damn." He rubbed the back of his neck with one big hand. "I didn't mean to imply...anything."

"It's okay." She looked away, placing the picture back

on the table. Whether he'd meant it or not, she was aware of the comparison.

"Uh, listen, it's getting late. Are you hungry? I could make us some sandwiches."

"Yes, I'm a little hungry." She welcomed the mundane subject of eating, a return to a safe area. "But you don't need to go to all that trouble. I could run pick up a pizza."

"No trouble. Come on into the kitchen and I'll show you how easy it is to throw something together around here."

He led her into the roomy, old-fashioned kitchen, opened the refrigerator and peered in. "You've got your choice of ham, turkey, corned beef or Spam sandwiches, hot dogs, hamburgers, nachos, even frozen pizza."

"I'm impressed. I think my refrigerator contains a few cartons of yogurt, and I'm not sure how old they are."

He leaned on the open door, looking back at her and grinning. "With a growing girl and assorted friends of that growing girl around, I keep a good supply of food in the house."

She flinched at the reminder that he had Kyla and she didn't, that he had a house and a refrigerator suitable for raising her daughter and she didn't.

Slowly his grin faded. "I've done it again, haven't I? I'm sorry. I'm not doing this on purpose. It's just that..." He shook his head. "I've never had to be careful what I say about Kyla. I don't know how to do that."

Distress clouded his eyes, but no dishonesty, no guile. Sam Woodward had no hidden agenda.

"I'm being too sensitive, reading criticism in everything you say." She smiled wryly. "When you do criticize, you're up-front and blunt about it. I'm well aware of that."

His grin returned. "Okay. Good. Now that we've got that straightened out, what'll you have for dinner?"

"I'd love a ham sandwich."

"White bread or wheat, mustard or mayonnaise, pickles, tomatoes, lettuce—"

She laughed. "You said this was going to be easy."

He sobered. "No," he said. "It isn't going to be easy. But we can do it."

The sandwich part, yes, but she wasn't so sure about anything beyond that.

A few minutes later, they sat at the table, drinking iced tea and eating ham sandwiches on paper plates and tortilla chips from the bag.

"How does your mother feel about your finding Kyla?" Sam asked.

"Excited about having a grandchild. Dying to meet her."

He stopped with his sandwich halfway to his mouth, poised to take another bite. "That's all?" he asked incredulously. "Not even a little guilty?"

She shrugged. "You'd have to know my mother. Her motives were pure as the driven snow. She wanted the best for me and for Kyla. She figures that makes everything all right."

He took another bite and chewed, watching her intently. His gaze made her nervous, filling her with a sudden need to defend her mother.

"She's a little overbearing, but she means well."

"Overbearing? Is that the same thing as domineering, a control freak?"

This was probably not the right time to ask if her mother could come to Kyla's birthday party. "Yes, all those things," she admitted. "But she did them because she loved me. My father died when I was eight, and she worked very hard to take care of me, to see that I had whatever I needed."

"Was she always so completely in charge of your life?"

Marcie picked up the top slice of bread on the remaining

half of her sandwich, then put it down again. Fidgeting. Avoiding Sam's gaze, his words.

"She was my mother. I did what she told me to. I was never a rebellious child."

"Until she told you to give up your baby."

She leaned back in the chair, abandoning any pretense at eating. "I couldn't do that. I wanted to please my mother, but I couldn't. I wanted my baby. You'd have thought I'd have been panic-stricken when I found out I was pregnant, seventeen and alone. But from the first time I realized it was a possibility, I was thrilled. I couldn't wait to hold my baby in my arms."

"You weren't worried about how you'd take care of her, support her?"

"Certainly I was worried. But I knew we'd manage. When my dad was alive, it never mattered that we didn't have a lot of *things*. I never even noticed the lack until after he died."

"So you thought you'd make up to your baby for all the love you didn't get from your mom after your dad died."

Marcie bristled. "Don't try to psychoanalyze me. I told you my mom did the best she could. Of course she loved me. In her own way. But that had nothing to do with the way I felt about my baby. You've never been pregnant. You don't know what it's like to carry a living person inside your body. It's a part of you and separate, and the love is so fierce and so strong, no man can even begin to imagine."

A sad longing settled in Sam's eyes, and Marcie regretted her outburst. "I guess not," he said quietly. "I love Kyla more than life itself, but it's different from the way Lisa loved her, from the way you love her. Not less, just different."

"I know," she admitted. "I didn't mean to get so carried away."

A tense silence stretched between them for a few seconds.

"What was he like, your dad?" Sam asked.

"Big and warm, like a friendly bear." Marcie smiled at the memory, the tension dissolving. "He laughed a lot. He'd come home from work and scoop me up in his arms, and he smelled like cherry pipe tobacco. He was a history teacher, and he thought he should smoke a pipe, even though he didn't particularly like it. But I did. I loved the smell, because it was his smell."

"How did he die?"

She ran her fingers down the side of her iced-tea glass, watching the moisture bead and roll away. "An aneurysm. He left one morning with a headache, then collapsed in his first class."

"You must miss him a lot." It was an observation, not a question.

"I did at first. It was a long time ago." *At least a lifetime.* "Do you still miss your wife?" Until she blurted out the question, she hadn't realized that she'd wanted to ask it for some time.

"After a while, the pain went away, but, yeah, I still miss her. Not all the time, but every once in a while, it sneaks up on me. I realize I've tossed a package of her favorite cookies into the basket at the grocery store, or something'll happen at school and I'll catch myself filing it away to tell her about later. I'm not sure we ever stop missing somebody we loved."

"You must have loved her a lot." She knew the answer, and didn't want to hear it, yet asked the question anyway.

Sam drained his tea and set the glass down with a rattle of ice cubes, then stared at it. "We were such kids." He lifted his gaze to hers. "Sure, we were in love, but our lives weren't really complete until Kyla came along. Lisa wanted a baby from the day we decided to get married. Almost like she knew she didn't have much time."

"You didn't want a baby?"

He shrugged. "I don't think men have the same maternal urges that women do. I wanted it because that's what Lisa wanted. At least until I felt the baby kick the first time." He smiled softly. "And when I held that squirming, red, wrinkled little girl, I completely lost my heart to her."

"Kyla." *Her* daughter.

"Marcie, I know it's hard for you to see anything good about losing your baby, but I don't think Lisa could have survived knowing her baby was dead. Kyla became her whole world. She was totally devoted to her. That was the happiest five years of her life."

And the saddest of mine, Marcie thought. She pushed away from the table and from her uncharitable feelings about a dead woman. "It's getting dark. Let me help you clean up so we can look at pictures and I can get out of here while you still have some of your Saturday night left."

"Not much to clean up. Do you want to pitch the paper plates or put the clip on the chips?"

Marcie carried the paper plates to the garbage can, then turned to watch Sam as he stored the chips and wiped off the counter. His ability to elicit such a range of emotions from her amazed and terrified her. Even beyond the heated desire his touch, his nearness and certainly his kiss evoked, he could set her every nerve on edge with a question or an offhand comment, then soothe her into complacent relaxation with a smile and a teasing remark.

She knew she couldn't let him do that. Her happiness, Kyla's happiness...it all depended on her ability to remain rational, in control, not so lost in Sam's touch, so susceptible to him, that she forgot to be careful. Never again would she trust her welfare to someone with a different goal from hers. Never again would she do something as stupid as what she'd done thirteen years ago, not demanding to see her baby when they told her the child had died.

"Okay, all clean," Sam announced. "Have a seat on the sofa, and I'll go drag out the mountains of pictures."

The smart thing would be to leave right now.

But she couldn't. She wanted desperately to see the missing years of her daughter's life.

And it didn't matter. Tonight, tomorrow, next week—she was tied to Sam for as long as he had her daughter.

Sam's sofa was big and old, and even though she tried to sit on the edge, she found herself sinking into the soft comfort, as if she were sinking into quicksand.

Chapter Nine

Sam hauled three albums and a box of loose photographs into the living room and set them on the coffee table in front of Marcie. She looked vulnerable and regal and altogether tantalizing as she tried and failed to sit primly on a sofa that could have swallowed Chicago.

Her eyes followed his actions, and she leaned forward to touch the albums almost reverently.

He sat beside her, cursing himself for his inability to keep in his thick head that she was here to see Kyla's pictures, not to see him. She herself had reminded him of that when she tried to explain a mother's love.

He'd never agree that she could possibly love Kyla any more than he did, but he had to agree that she obviously had a different kind of love, a kind so consuming and exclusive that she didn't even know he existed, except to carry in the pictures.

He dumped the box on the coffee table, the action abrupt, unnecessary and resulting in pictures spilling onto the floor. And it didn't even give him any release of tension.

Marcie leaned over and scooped up several, looking through them eagerly. "Oh, this one of her in the tree house is great." She held up a photograph taken a couple of years before. "Did you build it for her?"

"She and I built it together." He leaned closer to look at the picture of Kyla as she beamed at the camera and gave a thumbs-up sign. "She always wants to help. Look close here. See the black spot on the thumb she's holding up? She's not expressing her approval with that gesture. She's showing her war wound. She smashed it big-time hammering in a nail. I'm not sure whether she was prouder of the tree house or of her bruise."

Marcie leaned closer...to the picture and to him. Close enough that he could smell the light scent of flowers and rain.

She studied the spot he indicated, then lifted her gaze to his. And he was helpless to hold his emotions at bay. He had no choice but to join her in her pride and delight with Kyla. Marcie and he were two people bizarrely but irrevocably joined by love of two shared children...and at odds with each other as a result of that same love.

As though reading his thoughts, Marcie turned away and picked up another picture. "Dance recital?"

Sam laughed, groaned, and covered his eyes with one hand.

"She looks darling!" Marcie protested. "Those little blue tights, her hair up on her head and that red-and-white striped hat, that angelic smile...she's precious."

Sam leaned forward and took the photograph. "That was a night that went down in infamy."

"What happened? Did she miss a step or something? Perform stiffly? Freeze and couldn't go on? You shouldn't blame her for that. She's just a baby."

"Six years old." He shook his head. "Oh, no. She didn't

miss a step. Not one. And she sure didn't freeze up or
perform stiffly.''

"So what happened?"

Sam found himself suddenly reluctant to tell Marcie the
story, to let her take the memory.

But that was petty. Sharing the memory with Marcie
didn't mean he wouldn't still have it, too.

"About six months after Lisa died, George and Irene—
Lisa's parents—wanted Kyla to take dance classes. She
didn't want to. Even then she wanted to play baseball. But
I figured Irene knew more about being a mother than I did.
So off Kyla goes to dance class. At least, she went most
of the time, whenever she couldn't con me into letting her
skip.''

Sam warmed to his story, reliving the experience with
someone who felt his daughter was as wonderful as he did.

"Comes the recital, and everybody's there. George and
Irene, my parents, the parents of all the kids. Irene took
that picture before they went onstage. Look real close at
those eyes. Tell me if she looks more like an angel or an
imp. We should have known something was up. She was
being much too docile.''

Marcie's lips spread in a smile, anticipating Kyla's mis-
chief.

"So the curtain rises on these five sweet little girls. Everybody claps like mad, of course, then the taped music
starts, and they go into a tap routine. They're not doing too
badly, considering how young they are and how many
classes Kyla missed. They're not quite in sync, forget a
step here and there. Except Kyla. She dances like she's
inspired. Then all the little girls tip their hats. Kyla tosses
hers into the audience and launches into a pretty good imitation of a strip routine.''

"What?" Marcie's eyes widened, and her hands flew to her mouth.

"She'd seen it in some movie, and there she was, bumping and grinding and yanking the pins out of her hair. Fortunately, the teacher caught her just as she tugged one strap down her shoulder and winked at the audience."

Marcie burst into laughter. "What did Irene do?"

He rolled his eyes. "She was mortified. I think she wanted to disown both of us. But she never again suggested Kyla should take dancing lessons."

Marcie held the picture up again, her eyes full of pride and love. "What a little scamp she is."

"You don't know the half of it!" He leaned forward and reached for another picture at the same time she did. His shoulder touched hers, his hand connected with hers.

Connected. That was the right word, he thought as his gaze met hers.

Beneath his fingers, her skin was smooth and warm. He wanted to feel the rest of it, to run his hand up her slim arm, touch the ivory skin of her face, the full lips that were still faintly pink, even without lipstick.

She moved her hand away, and he began sorting haphazardly through the pictures. "You've got to see the one of her grade school graduation," he mumbled.

"Who's the little dark-haired girl?" Marcie asked, picking up more pictures from the floor. Only a slight quiver in her voice betrayed that she was as shaken as he by the accidental touch. Which was further proof that he'd better keep his hands and his hormones to himself. She might be attracted to him the way he was to her, but she had her priorities, and he wasn't on the list. "She looks like she might have Down's syndrome."

"She does. That's Melinda. When her parents tried to mainstream her into the regular school system, the other kids made fun of her. You know how cruel kids can be. Kyla was only eight then, but she took Melinda under her wing and dared anybody else to be mean to her.''

Marcie's eyes misted over. ''She's a very kind person.''

''She has a soft heart,'' Sam agreed. ''She can't stand to see anyone hurt.''

''I know so little about my own daughter,'' Marcie whispered.

Talk about a soft heart. He found himself wanting to share with her everything Kyla had said and done since they'd brought her home from the hospital.

''Would you mind very much if I borrow some of these pictures and have copies made?''

The minute she asked to take away part of Kyla, his erratic feelings switched abruptly to fear and resentment.

''Of course,'' she added hastily, ''if you don't want to let them out of your sight, I understand.'' He could only assume his thoughts had shown on his face. ''Maybe you could have copies made, and I could pay you for them....'' Her voice trailed off uncertainly.

''Pick out the ones you want and take them with you,'' he offered. ''You can get copies made at the same time as Jenny's pictures. I have some videos you can borrow, too.'' He had to throw in the last, go the extra mile to make up for his mental selfishness. Kyla always said she got her soft heart from him. Maybe she was right.

''Videos. That would be super.'' From the look on her face, anybody would have thought he'd just offered her a winning lottery ticket.

He turned his attention to the albums, the pictures Lisa had so carefully cataloged before her death. Selecting the one with the earliest dates on the spine, he hauled it into his lap. Might as well get on with it. She wanted as much of Kyla as she could have...and she was entitled to that.

Marcie watched Sam's big hands as they gently opened the album. From the chaos of the pictures in the box, she guessed that his wife had compiled the albums of earlier photos, neatly labeling each with the dates. The yearning inside her was a physical ache. It should have been her handwriting on the labels, her hands that placed the pictures of her daughter inside.

The first thing she saw when Sam opened the album was a photograph of a younger Sam in a tuxedo and a smiling, petite brunette in a white gown and veil.

"I'm sure you're not interested in our wedding pictures," he said, flipping quickly through the first few pages.

Actually, she was perversely fascinated. The images of Sam marrying someone, Sam kissing another woman, making love to her, swept over her with a paralyzing intensity, bringing the jolting realization that it wasn't only Lisa's place as a mother that she envied.

Before she could deal with the powerful feeling, Sam spread out before her pictures of Kyla as a baby—the way she'd looked the first time Marcie saw her, so long ago, and her attention was mercifully diverted.

"She's yawning! How adorable!"

"Yeah," Sam agreed. "She is."

"Trying to crawl at six months? She's precocious, isn't she?"

"Just busy. She had so many things to get into, she couldn't lie around in bed all day."

As she sat next to Sam, the album spread across both their laps, admiring Kyla's toothless grin and chubby legs, it almost seemed that they were two ordinary parents marveling at their daughter.

However, the intrusion of intermittent photos of Lisa cuddling Kyla and beaming maternally shattered that utopian fantasy. She was jealous of Lisa. Lisa had had Kyla's infancy. Yet at the same time, her heart went out to the pretty, happy woman who'd obviously loved Kyla so much and had to leave her so early. If Kyla couldn't have been with her real mother, Marcie was glad she'd had someone like Lisa.

Then Sam closed the first album and opened the next, exposing a studio portrait of Kyla's first birthday. Lisa held Kyla on her lap and Sam stood behind, one hand resting possessively on his wife's shoulder, smiling down at his family. The picture tugged painfully, reminding her of what she'd missed.

But the photograph beside it was the one that drew her as if it were a magnet. Lisa and Sam, holding hands and gazing devotedly into each other's eyes.

A hunger rose inside her, a hunger she could no longer ignore. She wanted Sam to look at her that way.

She was suddenly aware of his thigh pressing against hers as they sat beside each other. Had one of them moved closer? Surely they hadn't been sitting that way all along.

She didn't know. Her emotions had completely overpowered her brain.

Unable to stop herself, she looked up from the photograph to the reality. Sam's eyes widened then darkened, passion sparking in their depths. His nostrils flared slightly.

She ought to lower her gaze to the pictures. She ought to move away from him. She ought to get up and run from the house, get in her car, drive home and lock the door behind her.

But she was frozen in place.

No, *frozen* wasn't the right word. Of all the sensations shooting through her body, being frozen was certainly not one of them.

For a moment, she thought Sam might turn away and save them both.

Instead, he pulled her to him, his lips finding hers. The album slid from her lap as she twisted around and wrapped her arms about him, pressing her body close to his.

Out of control, she thought. *I am totally out of control.*

And then she stopped thinking and abandoned herself to sensation.

His lips were warm and soft, like the night coming through the open windows. His mouth moved against hers, sending tendrils of heat spreading through her body. His hands stroked her back, pressing her more tightly against his solid chest.

Any second now, she would pull away. She only wanted to enjoy the exquisite sensations one second more. For so long, she'd felt empty inside, and she hadn't even known it until Sam came along. Surely it would be all right if she indulged herself for a few more moments.

The tip of his tongue touched her lips, and she parted for him, taking a small portion of his body inside hers, reaching for and embracing the closeness.

She tangled her fingers in his unruly hair, wanting more of him, as much as she could have for as long as she could have it.

It was probably time to stop, she thought, but she couldn't quite remember why. His lips trailed down her throat, and her head tilted backward, a moan of pleasure escaping her own lips. His breath was warm on her skin, igniting everything it touched with fire that burned without consuming, and she ached to feel that fire on her breasts, her stomach, all over her body.

She slid her hands from his hair to his face. His stubble prickled her fingertips, and the sensation was unbearably erotic. His ruggedly masculine scent of hot summer and baseball games enveloped her, teasing her with worlds she'd forgotten existed.

He lifted his head, his eyes half-closed and smoky with desire, his breath coming in gasps that matched hers. With one hand, he cupped her cheek. "Marcie," he whispered, "we—"

The phone shrieked, cutting off whatever he'd been about to say.

He uttered a soft oath, then smiled. "Hold my place, okay?"

He moved to the end of the sofa and picked up the phone. "Hello?"

Marcie leaned back, drawing in huge gulps of air, trying to slow her racing heartbeat, the surging of her hormones. She couldn't decide whether she was upset or grateful for the interruption. Her body was definitely upset, but her mind protested at the ease with which she'd relinquished control to Sam.

It wasn't just the raging desire he inspired in her. That was certainly part of it, but it was everything else about Sam, about the whole day, that had allowed that desire to take over. The closeness that had begun at the carnival last week had intensified today at the cemetery, and all through the evening. They'd talked about themselves, revealing personal thoughts and feelings. She hadn't done that with anyone since Mitch. The last person she really trusted with herself had been her father. Until Sam.

After all that heady, unaccustomed closeness, the release of long-pent-up emotions, they'd looked at Kyla's pictures together and Sam had shared stories of her childhood.

She understood where Sam was coming from and felt that he understood her, and it felt good to be that free. Maybe he was right after all. Maybe they could do this, work through the labyrinth of complications together. Maybe it was safe to let down her guard and see where the passion that swelled between them would lead.

Sam hung up the phone and moved close to her again, a grin tilting the corners of his mouth, the same mouth that had so recently been on hers, that she wanted to feel on hers again. He draped an arm casually along the back of the sofa behind her, and a tingle darted through her body in anticipation of his touch.

"As you probably heard, that was our...my...that was Kyla," he said.

She smiled at his stumbling over the correct pronoun to describe whose daughter Kyla was. "Actually, I was thinking about something else and didn't hear a word."

"Well, you didn't miss much. She just called to see if she was right, that you were here with me."

"What did she say when you told her I was?"

He rolled his eyes. "She giggled. A lot. Said to be sure you were still planning to come to her party." He dropped his hand to her shoulder, gently urging her closer.

"I wouldn't miss it." She turned toward him, her fingers curving around the side of his neck, entranced by the warm flesh and the hard muscles and tendons beneath. "Oh, by the way, my mother wants to know if she can come."

Sam's entire body tensed. "Your mother wants to come to Kyla's birthday party, after what she did?"

Marcie withdrew her hand, regretting that she'd spoiled the delicious mood, yet aware that she needed to get this nagging problem out of the way. "I know. It wasn't my idea, but she really wants to meet Kyla."

Scowling, Sam pulled away from her, the physical action echoing the emotions she saw in his face. "No way. What kind of woman gives up her own granddaughter? I don't want that woman around Kyla."

"*That woman* happens to be Kyla's grandmother. You don't have the right to stop her from meeting her grandmother."

Sam was no longer the gentle man with lips that turned her to molten lava and arms she could gladly lose herself in, the man she'd easily entrusted with bits and pieces of herself. He was once again the man in control of her daughter, of her life.

Anger at his dictatorial attitude combined with fear that her daughter was slipping away from her...if she'd ever really had any part of her.

She regretted telling him about her personal life, allowing him to hold her and kiss her. Mostly, she regretted the reckless way she'd enjoyed all of it.

"I have the right to do whatever I want in my own house." Sam's voice was low and deadly. "Kyla doesn't even know who *you* are yet. I'm damned sure not going to bring in the grandmother who gave her away. Do you have any idea what kind of impact all this could have on her? I thought we agreed to get into this slowly, prepare her a little bit at a time, not throw in a hand grenade at her thirteenth birthday party."

Marcie shot to her feet. "*We agreed?* You dictated the terms, and I went along with them because I didn't have any other solutions. I want the best for my daughter, and I'll be the first to admit that I'm not at all certain what that might be. But I am certain of one thing. You don't know, either, so it's time you stopped making the rules."

Sam rose beside her and threw his arms into the air. "What rules? This isn't a game. There are no rules. We're just fumbling along, trying to do the best we can without totally messing up Kyla's life. What *rules* would you like to make?"

Marcie shook her head. She could have sworn the August night, so warm and soft before, had turned cold. She'd crept out of her safe corner into Sam's arms, and look where she'd ended up. On the outside looking in, not a part of Sam's life, or of Kyla's.

She'd allowed Sam to touch her deep inside, but she hadn't touched him. He was still her opponent, he was still someone she couldn't trust. He was still the one making decisions that involved *her* life, *her* daughter.

"I don't know what rules we should have, Sam," she said quietly. "I don't know how to do this, but I do know that somehow I'm going to reach my daughter. You've told me how much Lisa loved her. Well, I love her that much and more. She was once a part of me, and even though she's been a separate person since the moment I gave birth to her, that bond has never been broken, not when I thought she was dead, not when I heard her call you 'Daddy,' not when I saw pictures of Lisa holding her. I've already been through hell. Nothing you can say or do can stop me from reclaiming my daughter."

Sam's lips compressed to a thin line. "I understand."

The words, spoken starkly, yet with an underlying meaning she could only guess at, sent a chill down her spine.

"Since this is your house, I won't bring my mother to Kyla's party, but I will be here, and I want to tell her the truth."

"At her party?" He shook his head. "No. Forget it."

"Not at her party. But the next day. Next Sunday."

In the silence, Marcie was aware of every sound. A cricket outside burst into song, then stopped. A board somewhere in the old house creaked. A car passed in the street.

Sam looked tired, his hazel eyes dull. He drew in a deep breath, then turned away. "Fine. Next Sunday." He trailed the words behind him as he walked into the kitchen.

Marcie retrieved her purse and stared at the stack of pictures she'd selected to have duplicated. She left the house without them.

The air outside was warm after all. Humid and sticky, wrapping around her and threatening to stifle her.

She'd won. She'd made a decision, taken a stand. She ought to feel pleased, proud of her accomplishment.

Somehow, winning didn't feel any better than losing.

Chapter Ten

Music, happy voices and laughter floated through the open door and windows of Sam's house into the fading sunlight of the summer evening.

Marcie felt like an intruder as she went up the walk. Sam didn't want her at Kyla's birthday party. They hadn't spoken since she left last Saturday, but she was sure his attitude hadn't changed. Kyla might notice her absence if she didn't appear, but it wouldn't make any real difference.

Nevertheless, she had to go in. She had to face Sam, brave his anger as Demeter had braved the anger of the gods to reclaim Persephone, her only daughter.

She brushed imaginary lint from the skirt of her blue halter dress. Then, chin high, shoulders back, she took a deep breath and lifted her hand to knock on the screen door, to request admittance to the exuberant, noisy world where she had no place.

A boy about Kyla's age looked up, smiled and motioned her inside, then turned back to laugh at something his friend had said.

Marcie entered the room filled with strangers. Several people looked around and smiled but, when they didn't recognize her, turned back to their own conversations.

"Marcie!" Across the room, she saw Sam waving to her. He was smiling, too, but even from that far away, she could see that a cold distance had replaced the warmth in his eyes.

She made her way to where he stood with an older couple.

"George and Irene Kramer, this is Marcie Turner. George and Irene are Kyla's grandparents."

Lisa's parents. The people who thought they were Kyla's grandparents and would know differently after tomorrow.

Marcie felt deceitful as she shook hands with both of them. Irene was a tiny woman, her fingers birdlike and dry. George was as tall as Sam, but not as big. His smile and handshake were warm.

"Kyla told us all about you." Irene smiled softly. "I see you brought a gift." She looked up at Sam, as if waiting for him to make an announcement concerning her right to bring the gift.

He blushed, his rugged face turning a dark shade of red. "I'll go find Kyla. She's outside with her friends, burning the hot dogs."

"I'll go with you." She didn't want to be left alone with the Kramers, get to know them, see them as real people, feel sympathy for them in the loss of their daughter and now their granddaughter.

She started after Sam, but Irene's small hand on her arm stopped her. "Kyla speaks very highly of you. George and I are thrilled that Sam's finally shown an interest in someone. We lost our daughter, but we kept Sam as a son. He's a wonderful man. He deserves to be happy, and Kyla needs a mother. Lisa would want that."

Marcie blinked back hot tears and squeezed Irene's hand. She felt like a traitor in the midst of the good guys.

No, that wasn't right. *She* was the one who'd been wronged. *She* was the good guy.

But so were these people.

She turned away and hurried out the back door behind Sam.

Half a dozen kids Kyla's age were scattered around the backyard, perched on the picnic table or standing. One boy stood at the grill, brandishing a large barbecue fork. The smell of charcoal, hot dogs and hamburgers carried a sad poignancy, reminding Marcie of the other time she'd stood in this yard, so nervous, yet so full of hope, so certain everything would work out right, since she'd found her daughter.

How naive she'd been.

How different her mood was tonight.

How different Sam was tonight, avoiding her eyes, standing carefully apart from her. That first evening he'd been attentive, always beside her, touching her arm, her hand...kissing her good-night.

But only because he'd been pretending, for Kyla's sake, that she was his date.

Tonight there was no more need for pretense. Tomorrow the truth would be out in the open.

Suddenly she wasn't quite so eager for the truth to come out, for George and Irene Kramer to know they had no living grandchild, for Kyla to learn that Sam wasn't really her father, for the end of the pretense of being Sam's *friend.*

"Where's Kyla?" Sam asked the boy at the grill.

"Over there." He pointed to a tree at the edge of the yard. Kyla and Rachel sat beneath it, their heads together.

Sam strode toward them. Marcie followed, though he

hadn't asked her to, hadn't given any indication he ever knew she was there.

"Hi, Princess. Look who's here."

Kyla and Rachel raised their faces, Kyla's distressed and Rachel's streaked with dried tears. "Hi, Marcie," Kyla said. "I'm glad you came."

Sam sank down beside the girls. "Everything all right over here?"

Rachel burst into fresh tears, and Kyla gathered her friend into her arms. "Her dad married that woman," Kyla explained.

Rachel looked up and blew her nose on a shredded tissue. "He said she was my new m-mother." She sniffed and blew again.

Marcie took a fresh tissue from her purse, knelt in front of the girls and offered it to Rachel. Sam moved over, giving her plenty of room, avoiding any possibility of an accidental touch.

Rachel accepted the tissue. "Thank you. If you marry Coach, are you going to make Kyla call you 'Mother'?"

Marcie's stomach knotted, and she could feel the blood drain from her face.

Kyla looked from her to Sam.

"You'll always be free to call me whatever you want." Marcie made herself say the words that would reassure Kyla, ignoring the bottomless pit into which her heart had sunk at the thought that her daughter might never call her *Mother*. "Rachel, maybe you could talk to...your father's wife and see if you can agree on a nickname or something."

Rachel threatened to tear up again. "I hate her! I don' want to call her anything. She'll never take my mom' place!"

Marcie flinched. Would she be hearing those words from

Kyla tomorrow? "Of course she can't take your mom's place," she said, her voice coming out flat and lifeless. "If she doesn't know that by now, she'll figure it out. It'll be okay." *She'll figure it out, the way I did.* She could almost feel sorry for Rachel's stepmother.

"She won't figure it out. She's dumb and she's awful!" Rachel retreated to her tissue.

"She dyes her hair blond and wears a push-up bra that pushes her boobs right up out of her dress," Kyla said in an outraged tone.

"Kyla!" Rachel protested, sitting up straight and blushing furiously.

"Well, that's what you said."

"But I can't believe you told it in front of Coach!"

Sam leaned back against the tree. "I wish I'd been there to see that."

"Daddy!"

"The dyed blond hair! What'd you think I meant?"

Both girls giggled, and Marcie marveled at how easily he'd stepped in and dealt with the situation, turning tears into laughter.

"I think you have another birthday present here, you greedy girl," he said, indicating the package on the ground beside Marcie.

"Happy birthday." Marcie offered the gift to Kyla.

Kyla beamed. "Thank you!" She tossed aside the bow and ripped off the paper. "A music box! I love music boxes. How'd you know? Dad told you, didn't he?"

A warm glow started in Marcie's chest. "No, he didn't tell me. I loved music boxes when I was a little girl, and I thought you might, too."

Kyla lifted the porcelain carousel from its packaging. "Just like the carnival! I love it!"

Without hesitation, she handed it to Rachel. "You wind it up, and we'll see who can guess the song."

Rachel smiled, her pain for the moment beaten back by her friend's kindness.

Marcie's glow spread all over, and her eyes misted again. She wanted to lean against Sam, feel his arms around her while they shared the beauty of this wonderful, caring child they'd somehow produced between the two of them.

But, of course, she couldn't do that.

Sam moved up beside her, his shoulder touching hers as he leaned around to view the music box.

As Rachel held the carousel, lilting notes tingled through the evening, mingling with the happy sounds of the kids across the yard. "'Candy Man'!" both girls shouted at once.

Marcie wanted to look at Sam's face, to see if his touch was accidental or a peace offering.

If it was a peace offering, did she dare accept it? Did she dare trust him not to steal her happiness, the way her mother and Dr. Franklin had stolen it?

"Let's go show everybody," Kyla suggested. She started to rise to her feet, then stopped, leaned down and gave Marcie an impulsive hug. "Thanks! I love my music box!"

She and Rachel darted away to join the other kids.

Marcie was sure the glow inside had become so bright she'd light up the entire neighborhood. Her daughter had hugged her! The feeling of those slim arms about her neck, that smooth cheek pressed against hers, was a feeling she'd cherish forever.

"Marcie, don't you think we should talk?" Sam asked.

She sighed as reality filtered back in. "Yes," she agreed. "We have a lot to talk about."

She adjusted her position to sit face-to-face with him, far enough away that his nearness wouldn't muddle her thinking.

ing quite so much. If he wanted to talk, she had to have all her wits about her. She had to stay in control of herself, or she had no hope of controlling the outcome of this complicated situation.

Sam sat with one long, powerful denim-clad leg stretched out, the other foot on the ground, his arm resting on his bent knee. He was the sexiest man she'd ever seen, and just looking at him muddled her thinking.

"I wanted to call you all week," he said quietly, his gaze intent on her.

The release of tension in her stomach, the soaring sensation in her chest, told her how much she'd wanted to hear those words, how much she'd wanted him to call her.

He's only talking about the situation with Kyla, she warned herself. Even if he was talking about something different, something her heart wanted to hear, that *something* had no place in their lives right now. Ever since Sam agreed to tell Kyla, she'd obsessed about how they could possibly do it without upsetting her daughter. That was what they had to talk about.

"I wish you had called," she said. "I've felt terrible all week about our disagreement."

"Me too. I'm sorry I got so upset about your mom."

See? He only wanted to discuss the problems with Kyla, she told that foolish side of herself that kept reading in meanings that weren't there. "You had every right to be upset. Believe me, I'm upset with her, too. If she wasn't my mother... But she is. I have to get along with her."

He nodded. "I understand. What did she say when you told her she couldn't come tonight?"

"She was hurt. She got all teary. She's really not a bad person. She wants to do things right. It's just that her methods are questionable."

"Her methods suck."

Marcie gave a short laugh. "For a football coach, you sure have a way with words."

One corner of Sam's mouth tilted up in a small half smile. "We don't have a lot of time on the football field for excess words. We have to get right to the point. And I guess the point is, right now I think this should be between you, me and Kyla. We've got a ton of problems to work through before we let anybody else bring in their problems."

Marcie thought of the way Kyla had looked from her to him at the idea of calling her Mother. She nodded. "You're right. The Kramers, my mother, the rest of the world that's going to be involved in the ripple effect will have to stand in line. The most important person in this drama—this tragedy—is Kyla."

Sam watched the shifting emotions play across Marcie's face like the shadows and light from the dying sun filtering through the tree above.

"Yes," he said, "Kyla is the most important person. But what about *us?*"

The question had been on his mind so much the past week, it came out even though Marcie had just underscored what he already knew, that Kyla was the only one who mattered, that there was no *us*. Marcie was drawn to him, he could tell that from the way she looked at him with desire and need in her eyes, from the way she'd kissed him last Saturday night, from a thousand little things. But it wasn't enough, not for her and certainly not for him.

"Us?" She spoke the word so softly, it seemed to be part of the evening breezes whispering through the leaves above them.

"You realize, once we tell Kyla the truth, there won't be any reason to keep pretending we're having a relationship."

"No. I don't suppose there will be."

"I'm going to miss it."

"We'll always have a relationship through Kyla."

"That's not what I meant." *Shut up, Sam!* he ordered himself. She'd made her position clear. To her, he was Kyla's father. That was all.

That was what her words told him, but not her eyes. He knew those eyes. He'd seen them in his daughter's face every day for the past thirteen years. After all that time, he knew how to read them. Marcie could no more hide her feelings from him than Kyla could.

And Marcie's eyes contradicted her words. Marcie's eyes were brimming with unspoken passion and deep emotions.

He reached for her hand, and she placed it in his.

"I can't," she said, her words contradicting her actions.

The back door slammed, and Marcie jerked away.

"Kids," Sam grumbled.

"Daddy!"

He looked up to see Kyla racing toward him, her face pale, her eyes wide and panic-stricken.

He and Marcie both stood. Marcie's expression mirrored Kyla's, but Sam noted that Kyla wasn't bleeding or limping, so it couldn't be too bad. Marcie just hadn't learned yet that everything was a major crisis to kids of Kyla's age.

He caught her as she threw herself into his arms. "It's okay, Princess." He patted her back. "Daddy's here. Tell me what happened."

"Her mother said—" She tightened her grip around his neck, as if holding on for dear life.

"Rachel's mother?"

"No." She pushed away, but still hung on to his arms. Her lips were quivering, and her eyes were suspiciously moist. He recognized her I'm-a-big-girl-now routine. Whatever had her so upset, she was determined not to cry about it. "Marcie's mother."

He froze.

Marcie gasped. "What about my mother?"

Kyla kept her gaze focused on him, refusing to look at Marcie. "She said terrible things."

Waves of anger, terror and sorrow slammed against Sam. He didn't have to ask, *What terrible things?* He couldn't ask, anyway. His throat muscles were paralyzed.

"My mother called you?" Marcie exclaimed.

A man's voice interrupted them. "Sam!"

Sam looked toward the back door, to see George standing on the top step.

"You all need to come in here for a minute." Though his father-in-law was obviously trying to keep his tone calm, Sam could hear the strain in his voice.

"Yeah, Daddy, come talk to that woman and make her quit saying those things."

That woman? The words bounced through Marcie's chest like a lead ball as she followed Sam and Kyla across the yard. Rachel's words to describe her stepmother.

But Kyla wasn't talking about Marcie. She was talking about Marcie's mother, the woman who'd stolen her daughter and wrecked her life once.

And now she was doing it again.

The ground seemed to sway, to move beneath her feet, up and down and sideways, threatening to trip her, to suck her under, to toss her off. Even the earth had lost its stability.

She'd told her mother not to interfere, ordered her to stay away from the party, from Kyla, not to call her or in any way contact her. She'd tried her damnedest to take back her life.

And it hadn't worked.

"They're up in Kyla's room." George held the screen door open for Sam and Kyla to go through the kitchen, but he looked at Marcie uncertainly, as though he couldn't decide if she should be allowed entrance.

She took the door from him and went in, determinedly following Sam and Kyla through the crowd and upstairs, but stopping in the doorway of Kyla's room.

Her mother, a petite woman with short auburn hair glued into a no-nonsense style, stood beside a window, the white ruffled curtains an inappropriate background.

George pushed past her and went to sit beside his wife on the bed. Irene had little more color than the white spread that matched the curtains.

Kyla's room was light and airy, but the atmosphere was turbulent.

"What are you doing here, Mother?" she demanded.

"That's a damned good question," Sam said, holding Kyla close. "I thought you told her not to come."

"She really is your mother?" Kyla asked. It was the first thing Kyla had said to her since she rushed into the backyard. Of course she'd turned for comfort to the father who'd raised her, not some woman she'd just met, even though that woman happened to be her mother.

She was not a part of Kyla's life.

Nor was she a part of Sam's.

And that last part hit just as hard as the first.

She had no more control over her emotions than she did anything else in her life. She cared for Sam. It wasn't smart. It wasn't planned. But as much as she wanted Kyla for her daughter, she wanted Sam for her friend, her lover, just as much.

Actually, she realized, she'd felt that way about him for some time, but hadn't been able to admit it to herself. Now, with the rest of the world falling apart, loving Sam didn't seem such a terrible thing.

Her mother moved into the center of the room. "I'm trying to help you, sweetheart. You're just like your father. You're too soft. You never could take charge and make decisions. I've always had to make them for you."

Marcie forced her voice to be calm. "Let's step into the hall and talk about this, Mother."

"Not now, dear. I want to get to know my granddaughter." She turned to Kyla with a smile and stroked her hair. Kyla nestled closer to Sam.

"I'm not your granddaughter. Go away!"

Marcie flinched at Kyla's rejection of Anne as if it had been a rejection of her. "Please come out here with me for a minute, Mother."

Anne flashed a smile to the room at large and shrugged. "I never could deny my daughter anything."

She walked into the hall, and Marcie closed the door behind them, walling herself and her mother away from the people they'd hurt.

Anne whirled on Marcie. "This is your fault. If you'd done what I told you in the first place, made that man tell Kyla the truth weeks ago, we wouldn't have to have a big scene now. My own granddaughter would know who I am."

"If I'd done what you told me to?" Marcie exclaimed, the last vestige of control leaving her. But it had never done her any good, anyway. "When did I ever stop you from getting your way? Even when I tried to go against you, to keep my baby, you lied and took her from me! You've always managed to win!"

A long-suffering look on her face, Anne reached for Marcie's arm, but Marcie jerked free. "No! You've got to leave me alone. Let me make my own mistakes. They can't be any worse than the ones you've made for me.''

Tears welled up in Anne's eyes. "I can't believe the way you're talking to me. I worked two jobs to support you after your dad died. I gave you everything I could, more than your dad gave you when he was alive. And this is the thanks I get.''

Marcie had heard the words too many times. They no longer raised her level of guilt to the drowning stage. "You didn't give me more! We were happy when Dad was alive. He loved me. That's the one thing you never gave me after he died.''

Anne's face crumpled, lines usually hidden by careful makeup folding in on themselves. She held out both hands beseechingly. "I did the best I could for you. I did all I knew how to do. I did it because you're my daughter, and I love you. Just the way you love your daughter.''

It was the first time Marcie had ever seen her mother genuinely vulnerable. She wanted to go to her, put her arms around her and forgive her, but she couldn't. Not until she talked to Kyla, not until she discovered the extent of the damage. "If you loved me so much, how could you not know how much I loved my daughter, how much I wanted her?''

"She's had a good life. You can see that.''

"Better than I could have given her?'' she demanded quietly. "Go on home, Mother. We'll talk later.''

"I'll call you tomorrow.''

Marcie nodded, then opened the door to go back in and face the results of her mother's brand of love.

As she entered, silence rushed at her.

Kyla, sitting on the bed between Irene and Sam, hung on to her father's arm with one hand and pleated the edge of her shorts with the other, refusing to meet Marcie's gaze.

George and Irene both seemed to have aged ten years, while Kyla looked much younger, her almost-grown-up self-confidence gone.

"I explained everything to them," Sam said. His face had turned to stone, the tendons in his granite jaw standing out. "Kyla knows you're her mother."

Kyla looked up, anger and fear fighting for ascendancy on her tearstained face. "Why are you doing this? I thought you were my friend."

Had there ever really been a time when Marcie was eager for this? Rather than a beginning, this felt like an ending.

Chapter Eleven

Sam clenched his jaw and fought to remain rational, to survive the tide of emotion enveloping everyone in the room. Irene had a weak heart, just like her daughter and granddaughter, and he wasn't sure how much she could take. Kyla had just received the biggest shock of her young life.

And, of course, there was Marcie. Marcie, who'd caused it all.

No, he contradicted himself. Marcie had simply tried to undo what her mother had done. She was as much a victim as the rest of them.

"Lisa's baby's dead," Irene said in a weak, quavery voice.

"Yes, she is," Sam confirmed, fighting the tightening in his throat that threatened to cut off his voice. "I'll take you to her grave when you're ready."

George patted Irene's hand. "It's all right, Mother. It's all right."

Irene shook her head. "Our Lisa's baby died. And

now..." She looked fearfully at Marcie. "Now we're losing our Kyla."

Sam could feel Kyla's small body begin to convulse with sobs she fought to keep inside.

"No," Marcie protested. She made a move to approach Irene, but then drew back, edging closer to the door, as if seeking distance from everybody. "You're not losing Kyla. She'll always be your granddaughter."

Sam held his breath, praying the Kramers wouldn't say something to hurt Kyla more than she'd already been hurt, something about her not really being their grandchild. People sometimes said thoughtless things at moments of crisis.

"Thank you," George murmured. He stood and urged Irene upward. "Come on, Mother. Let's head back home. I think we need to get away and sort this all out."

They both gave Kyla a hug as they were leaving, and Sam dared to breathe again. One hurdle successfully scaled.

"Call us tomorrow?" George asked as they left.

"I will," Sam promised.

Now only he, Kyla and Marcie remained. The *truth* Marcie had wanted for so long stared back at them, swirled around them like the blackness of night through the open windows.

"Why don't you sit down?" he suggested. He motioned Marcie to the chair in front of Kyla's desk. She pulled it out, the legs scraping loudly across the wooden floor.

Marcie flinched at the noise.

"It always does that. I need to put rubber tips on it." He clutched at this small, mundane piece of his former world as if it might somehow pull them back. Of course, it couldn't.

Kyla held on to him desperately, the way she'd held on after Lisa died.

"I'm so sorry, Kyla." Marcie sat rigidly in the chair, hands clenched in her lap. "I never wanted you to be hurt."

Over the top of his daughter's head, Sam looked at her, and for the first time, they were on the same team.

"We both love you, Princess. There's no way either of us can change what's happened, but we'll do anything we can to help you accept it."

"That woman didn't want me. She gave me away."

"I did want you!" Marcie leaned forward, hands stretched futilely toward Kyla, her delicate features contorted in agony. "I wanted you more than anything in the world! I've loved you all these years even when I thought you were dead."

Kyla lifted her head and looked at Marcie. "I didn't mean you," she said quietly. "I meant that grandmother woman."

Tears slid silently down Marcie's cheeks, and Sam wasn't sure whether they were tears of sorrow or tears of relief that Kyla didn't blame her. "It wasn't that she didn't want you. My father died when I was small, and it was tough for her to raise me alone. She thought you'd have a better life with a mother and a father."

"Are you going to marry my dad?"

Marcie's face flushed bright red.

"Marcie and I aren't really dating," Sam explained. "We thought we could make all this easier to deal with if you got to know Marcie gradually."

Kyla turned to him. "You lied to me?" Accusation and hurt frayed the edges of her voice.

"No, not really. Well, sort of, I guess. We just didn't tell you all the truth. I mean, Marcie *is* my friend. Our friend."

Kyla shook her head. "You didn't tell the truth. You've always told me that's the same as a lie."

"You're right. It is. We deceived you. I'm sorry. Marcie wanted to tell you everything immediately, but I didn't think we should."

"I wish you'd never told me." She burrowed her head under his arm, the way she'd done as a child when something frightened her.

"Nothing's going to change," Marcie said. "The only difference will be one more person in your life who loves you." She gave a small, shaky smile. "Me."

"Daddy, if she's my... I mean, are you still..." She hiccuped back a sob. "What about my real mother? My first mother? If she wasn't my mother, then you're not—"

"Of course I'm still your father."

"You can't be, if she's—" She shook her head, refusing to acknowledge Marcie as her mother.

"Yes, he can!" Marcie slid from the chair and knelt beside the bed. She reached up to embrace Kyla, then dropped her hands, as if unable to try, for fear of rejection. "It takes more than an accident of birth to make a parent. Lisa took care of you and loved you when you were a baby, until the day she died. Your dad's raised you and loved you all your life."

Kyla sat up and turned toward Marcie. "You haven't. I just met you," she said accusingly.

Marcie's head dipped as if she'd been struck.

"Marcie never had a chance to do all that," Sam defended. "Can't you give her that chance now?"

Kyla wiped her eyes with her wrist and didn't answer.

"Will you think about it?"

She nodded without looking at him. It was the best he could expect under the circumstances.

"Attagirl. Why don't Marcie and I go down and tell everybody the party's over, then the three of us, or just you and I, whichever you want, can talk about this all night?"

She shook her head again. "I want to go talk to Rachel."

Marcie looked at him for confirmation of the wisdom of that action. "Okay, Princess. You go talk to Rachel, but anytime you're ready, you let me know, and I'll take down my shotgun and get rid of all these wild party people."

She stood, avoiding Marcie, and made her way to the door then looked back. "I love you, Daddy."

"I love you, too, Princess."

She left, closing the door behind her.

"Will she be all right?" Marcie asked, looking up at him, her face a study in anguish.

He drew in a deep breath, exhaling on a long sigh. "Probably. Eventually."

"Should we let her go off alone like that?"

He nodded. "It's part of growing up. She wants to talk to her friends instead of her parents."

"I see." She shook her head. "I don't know anything about my daughter. I didn't know what to say, how to make it better. This wasn't the way I wanted it to be."

He laid a hand on her slim shoulders, unable to control the need to touch her. He wanted to pull her into his arms, give and receive comfort, the way a typical mother and father did when they'd been through a crisis with their child.

But, of course, they weren't a typical mother and father. Whatever their relationship was, it wasn't typical.

For a long moment, they gazed into each other's eyes. Then he reached for her, and she surged upward into his arms.

"It was awful!" she whispered, holding on to him frantically. "I feel awful, empty and scared, scared for Kyla because she's so hurt and so confused, and scared for me because she won't admit I'm her mother and I don't know how to be a mother anyway—and the only thing that feels good is being in your arms.''

"Shh..." He placed a finger on her lips, then replaced it with his mouth, seeking a refuge from the horror of the past hour in the soul-cleansing ecstasy of Marcie's kisses, of holding Marcie so tightly against him that he could almost believe she was a part of him and the one of them was a wall against the rest of the world.

Marcie gave herself up totally to the power of Sam's kiss. This wasn't what she'd meant to do when she threw herself into his arms. Or maybe it was. Maybe this was the only thing that could assuage the ache from all that had just happened, the only thing that could fill the emptiness.

His lips moved on hers, bringing strength and courage, lifting her above the pain and worry, making her aware of him and of her and of the pleasures of the blending.

Her breasts, flattened against his chest, tingled with awareness. His hand caressed her neck, his fingers weaving into her hair, pushing aside the horrors of the night, taking her to a place of light and safety.

His lips slid from her mouth down her throat. "I need you, Marcie," he whispered, his voice and his breathing ragged. "I don't know how I can survive if I don't have you."

This, she thought, was what making love was all about. Not the hurried, frenetic coupling that had produced Kyla, but a deep need to drown in each other.

She tangled her fingers in his hair. She wanted to tell him that she loved him, that she wasn't sure when it had happened, that it had crept over her slowly, probably beginning with the moment he raced up to her car window and looked in with such concern on his rugged features. She wanted to tell him, but words seemed inadequate and inappropriate at that moment.

Nothing mattered right now but exploring and luxuriating in the glorious feeling of touching Sam, tasting his lips, smelling his football-coach scent that blended with the summer scents of green leaves and grass coming through the window.

Brakes and tires screamed from the street below, followed by a thud and loud voices.

"Kyla!" someone cried. "Help! She's dead!"

Heart trying to come up her throat, Marcie sprinted toward the door with Sam beside her.

"Somebody's talking *to* Kyla, not about her!" Sam shouted as they took the stairs two at a time.

He had to be right. Marcie couldn't accept any other explanation.

They raced through the house, pushing aside guests who got in their way, out to the street, to where Rachel knelt beside a still form.

"Oh, God!" Sam sank to the pavement. "Kyla! Baby! It's Daddy! Say something! Open your eyes! Look at me!"

Marcie whirled around and started back to the house to call for help.

From the black car that loomed only a few feet away, a man jumped out and ran to stand over Kyla. "I called for an ambulance on my cell phone! They said don't move her! Oh, God, I'm so sorry! I didn't see her! I turned the corner and she ran right in front of me!"

Feeling completely useless, Marcie knelt beside Sam and laid a trembling hand on her daughter's pale cheek.

"Don't die, baby! Please don't die again." Her tears fell on the pavement, and she didn't try to stop them.

"She won't die," Sam said, his words broken by sobs. "I won't let her."

But she knew what he said didn't matter. His attempts at control were as futile as hers. No matter how hard she tried, she had no control over anything, not her tears or her life or even her baby's life.

Marcie sat beside Sam on the vinyl sofa in the impersonal visitors' room of McAlester Regional Hospital while they waited for Kyla to get out of surgery...while they waited to find out if she'd live or die.

The similarity between this room and the one where they'd sat together awaiting the results of the genetic testing seemed a cruel parody. How foolishly naive she'd been, thinking she could somehow straighten out the twists in her life and make everything right.

Sam raked a hand through his perpetually tousled hair. His eyes were red and swollen from intermittent surges of tears. "She's going to be all right," he said, for perhaps the hundredth time. Marcie didn't believe him any more than she'd believed him when they knelt beside Kyla's motionless body, waiting for the ambulance.

"It's my fault," she said dully. Her pain went beyond screaming, beyond tears, beyond her ability to express. She could only speak in a monotone devoid of all emotion. "If Kyla hadn't been so upset, she wouldn't have been so careless. She wouldn't have run into the street without looking."

Sam shook his head and leaned forward, resting his forearms on his knees. His gaze focused on the door, avoiding her. "It's not your fault. Kyla and Rachel darted into that street without looking, just like Kyla did the first day you came by the house, when you almost hit her. If anybody's to blame, it's me. I promised Lisa I'd take care of Kyla, and I didn't do it. I've failed her as a father."

"Oh, Sam, don't say that! You're a wonderful father!"

Sam shook his head again. "When Lisa was alive, she was with Kyla every second. She never let her out of her sight. Kyla was her whole world. She even moved a cot into Kyla's room so she could be with her when she slept. At the time, I resented being shut out of her life. I didn't think she needed to be that protective, but she did. This proves it.''

Marcie listened in astonishment to this description of Sam's wife. ''That doesn't sound normal,'' she protested.

He looked at her then, agony filling his eyes and spilling down his tanned cheeks. ''Isn't it? Don't you want to do the same thing, be with her, take care of her, keep her safe?''

''Yes, I guess I do. But—'' *Moving out of Sam's bed? Shutting him out of her life?* If Sam was a part of her life, if she and Sam and Kyla were a family, she could never do that. No matter that she loved her daughter more than life itself. That was also how much she loved Sam.

''Sam,'' she said quietly, needing to relieve some of his pain, even if she couldn't find any relief from hers, ''you can't take responsibility for everything that happens in this world. You can't control life or death or what other people do. When you try, that's when you cause problems. My mother thought she could make my life and my baby's turn out better, and look what that caused. Then I thought I could fix things, and it only got worse. We can't control anything, not for good or bad. When you love somebody, you've got to let go of that person, let him or her make his choices and succeed or fail without you.''

Sam's gaze searched her face for several long moments. Then he rose slowly, pulling her up with him and into his arms.

''I couldn't get through this if you weren't here with me,'' he whispered, his warm breath touching her hair.

There wouldn't be anything to get through if I hadn't interfered, she thought, but she let herself sink into the warm, blissful haven of Sam's arms, to enjoy the gratitude she had no right to enjoy, to feel the ecstasy of Sam's body pressed against hers.

"Mr. and Mrs. Woodward?"

She and Sam whirled apart at the sound of the voice. A doctor in surgical scrub clothes stood in the doorway, pulling off his blue paper hat.

"How's Kyla?" Sam asked, one arm still around Marcie, supporting her or supporting himself. She couldn't tell which, but she was infinitely grateful. Her legs were suddenly so shaky, she knew she couldn't stand alone.

"Are you her parents?" the doctor asked.

"Yes," Sam said without hesitation. "I'm her father, and this is her mother. How is she?"

"She's going to be fine."

A dam burst inside Marcie, and she wanted to laugh and cry at the same time. Sam held her more tightly against his side while the doctor gave them a technical recitation of what he'd done. She heard a word here and there—*concussion, broken leg, torn ligaments, fractured ribs*—but for the most part, what he said flew past her, completely obscured by that one sentence, *She's going to be fine.*

Then she froze in terror as one terrible phrase caught her attention.

"...lost her—"

"What?" she demanded. "What did you say?"

"At one point, we thought we'd lost her," he repeated, "but then her vital signs came back stronger than before." He smiled. "You've got one determined daughter there. She's in recovery now. Why don't you folks go grab some breakfast, and by the time you get back, she'll be awake and in her room and you can go see her."

He left, and she and Sam stood locked together.

"She made it," Sam said cautiously.

"So close. We came so close to losing her."

Sam turned her to face him and tilted her chin upward with one finger. As he smiled, the sun rose in his eyes bringing back the sunbursts at the corners. "Close only counts in horseshoes. She made it. Our daughter made it."

Our daughter made it. For the first time, it registered that Sam had told the doctor she was Kyla's mother, that he'd referred to her as *our* daughter.

He stepped over to a window, raised the blinds and looked out.

"It's almost dawn. It's a new day, and Kyla's going to make it. Let's go get some breakfast and talk about what we're going to do with this new day, where we go from here, how we can help Kyla handle all this."

Sam was inviting her into his and Kyla's life, and never had Marcie felt more like an outsider.

Her determination to reclaim her daughter had wilted. Her insistence had almost resulted in her losing her daughter forever, and had totally changed the life of the man who'd loved and raised Kyla, the man she herself loved. Had she turned into her mother, determined to move heaven and earth to have things her own way, no matter who got hurt in the process?

She didn't want to give Kyla the painful, destructive kind of love her mother had given her.

She'd realized earlier that night that she loved Sam, though events had happened too fast after that for her to have time to deal with that realization. A few minutes ago, as he held her, as he included her in his family, that love had swollen to epic proportions.

Now, as she watched him turn from the window to her, the promise of tomorrow in his eyes, she knew the time had come to decide what she was going to do about loving him, about loving Kyla. Her life had been safe but empty until Kyla and Sam came along. Now her heart brimmed with love, but it hadn't made her or the people she loved any happier.

"I need to freshen up just a little bit first," she said. "There's a ladies' room right down the hall. I'll be back in a few minutes."

"Good idea. I could stand to throw a little water on my face, too."

He followed her down the hall, to a separate door.

"Meet you back in the visitors' room that did *not* get the *Good Housekeeping* seal of approval," he said with a tired grin.

Marcie went over to the sink, splashed cold water on her face and dried her hands. Then she stood gazing into the water-spotted mirror for a long time, looking into her own eyes, trying to sort through her thoughts and emotions, to separate reality from fantasy.

Her appearance in her daughter's life had been selfish and destructive. She'd hurt Sam and Kyla, the two people she loved most in the world. She had to try to undo the harm she'd done. She had to back away, let them try to rebuild their lives, find the happiness they'd had before she showed up.

And she had to try to return to the detached peace she'd known before. She should never have left her safe corner. Could she ever find her way back?

Finally she took a small notepad from her purse, the same notepad on which Sam had written his phone number that first day she drove by their house.

Dear Sam, she wrote, thinking how appropriate it was that this episode should end with a letter from her, as it had begun with one from Dr. Franklin to her.

Chapter Twelve

The pain in Sam's back woke him with a start.

He'd fallen asleep in one of the uncomfortable chairs in the visitors' lounge at the hospital.

He rubbed the stubble on his chin and wondered what was taking Marcie so long.

Then he saw the folded pieces of paper on his lap. Someone must have put them there while he was asleep.

He unfolded them and stared in confusion at the tidy, precise handwriting. His eyes scanned to the signature on the second page.

Marcie

Why was she leaving him a note?

Dear Sam:

I don't want to do to Kyla what my mother did to me. I don't want to ruin her life with that possessive, controlling kind of love.

He rubbed the sleep from his eyes and tried to clear the fog from his head. What the hell was she talking about?

When I found out I was pregnant, I thought I'd have someone to love and be loved by. My life was pretty lonely after my dad died. Then when Jenny died, too, I found a safe, empty spot in my heart and hid there for years...until you and Kyla came along. But in trying so hard to make things come out right this time, I hurt my daughter, physically and emotionally and I wrecked your life. You're the two people I care about most in the world, and I've hurt you both.

I don't know how to be a mother. I gave birth to Kyla and I love her with all my heart, but I could never be the kind of mother to her that Lisa was, and I don't want to be the kind of mother my mom was to me. Even though you had no part in her conception, Sam, you're a wonderful father. I trust you with my daughter, so I'm leaving her in your care.

You were a happy family until I came long. If I disappear from the picture, maybe you can get things back to the way they were before I blundered in and ruined everything.

If there ever comes a time...and I pray there will...when Kyla wants to get to know me, you know where to find me. It's too late for me to be Kyla's mother, but maybe someday I can be her friend. Maybe someday, when all this is far behind, I can be your friend.

Disbelieving, Sam read the note a second time, then crumpled it angrily and threw it across the room.

After all they'd been through this past night, how the hell could she do something like that? They'd been there for each other, comforted each other, shared their fears and their hopes and, finally, their joy. They'd done it all together, with Kyla their focus, but not to the exclusion of each other, not the way it had been with Lisa.

A triangle. That was what he'd thought they were, with Kyla at the top, supported by both of them, while they held firmly to each other. While they loved each other.

At least he'd thought they loved each other.

The words hadn't been spoken, and he wasn't even sure when he'd known how he felt about Marcie. But sometime during that awful night, he'd known he loved her, wanted her in his life always, as his wife, as Kyla's mother. And he'd thought she felt the same.

Well, he'd been wrong. They were a triangle with no base, no connection between Marcie and him except through Kyla. She loved his daughter. That was the love he'd mistaken for belonging to him. He'd been right about that all along.

He crossed the room, picked up the wadded note and threw it again, then swore under his breath. He needed something more solid to throw. He needed to hit a punching bag, to run twenty laps around the football field, something to drain the anger and frustration Marcie's note had left him with.

He yanked the blinds closed, no longer wanting to see the pale fingers of sunlight bringing a new day.

His daughter was going to be fine, and half of his heart was filled with indescribable joy, but the other half was dark as the night they'd just gone through. How could he have been so wrong about Marcie?

Against his will, he thought about the way they'd held each other, the way she'd responded to his kisses.

What if he hadn't been wrong about her?

He snatched up the note, spread it out and scanned it

again. ...*safe, empty spot in my heart...until you and Kyla came along... ...the two people I care about most in the world... ...I wrecked your life.* She was leaving so that he and Kyla could reclaim their earlier happiness...and so that she could reclaim that safe, empty spot, safe not just from the pain of Kyla's rejection, but also from the possibility of his?

She trusted him with the daughter she adored. Those were not the words of a woman who didn't care.

Maybe Lisa wouldn't have been so obsessed with Kyla if he'd fought harder for their relationship...if he'd loved her as desperately as he loved Marcie.

Well, this time he was going to fight. He was going to try, even if he got knocked down for his efforts.

With a scowl, he turned back to the window again. The light coming in around the edges of the blinds wasn't much brighter than when he'd checked before he and Marcie went to freshen up. He couldn't have slept long, not more than a few minutes.

Marcie might still be in the hospital. They'd ridden over in the ambulance. She'd have to call a taxi to get to his house for her car, and there was a better-than-average chance it hadn't arrived yet.

He bolted from the room and charged over to the elevator.

As he strode across the main lobby downstairs, he saw her standing on the walk just outside. The light blue summer dress that had looked so fresh yesterday evening, when he first saw her at Kyla's party, was rumpled and wilted...like her. The night had taken its toll on both of them.

She looked up, startled, when he pushed open the door.

Marcie bit her lip as Sam charged out the door toward her. An irrational surge of happiness at the sight of him battled with fear for the safety of her precariously perched emotions. "Hi," she said, smiling unsurely.

He thrust the crumpled note toward her. "Do you want to explain this?"

"You were asleep. I didn't want to wake you."

"That's not even a good explanation of why you left me a note and walked away, much less a good explanation of what you said in this note."

"I don't know any other way to explain it. I'm trying to understand it myself. I only know I don't want to hurt Kyla or you any more."

For several seconds, they stood in silence, staring at each other, inches and miles apart.

A taxi pulled around the drive and stopped.

"Goodbye, Sam." She turned to leave, knowing that if she stayed one more minute, she would completely lose the courage to go.

He took her arm, halting her, his touch erasing the last of her strength. The only way she could leave now would be if he told her to.

"If you don't want to hurt us, then don't leave us. You're right about one thing. Giving birth doesn't automatically make you a mother. Look at your own mother. But love does. You love Kyla, and, given time, she'll love you. Give her that time."

"That's up to Kyla."

"Damn it, Marcie, you're the most frustrating woman I've ever met. Stay here. I'll be right back." He strode over to the taxi, gave the driver some money and sent him away.

She watched him, knowing she should protest, she should get in that taxi and leave, avoid putting Sam and Kyla…and herself…through any more pain.

He came back to her. "Okay, we check with Kyla on that. But what about us?"

"Us?" Her heart began to hammer as he repeated the question he'd asked the evening before, the question they'd left hanging to deal with the crisis of her mother's intrusion at Kyla's party.

"Yeah, us. The *us* that share two children. The *us* that can't keep our hands or our lips off each other. The *us* that need each other to survive, to be complete. You can't go back to hiding like you did all those years."

"I'm not going to—" She stopped in the middle of her protest. That was exactly what she'd planned to do, and she couldn't deny it with Sam's hazel eyes boring into hers.

"Yes, you did. But you can't do that, any more than I can go back to my life before you came along, the way you said I should in this note." He waved the wrinkled papers at her. "Everything's changed. Both our lives have changed, and we can't undo that, even if we wanted to. You moved into my life and into my heart, and I don't even want to go back."

He lifted a big hand to cup her chin, his fingers tenderly stroking her cheek. "I didn't know it at the time, but something was missing. Now I've found that missing something. I love you, Marcie, and I'm not going to let you run away and hide from that love."

He was saying what she wanted desperately to hear, promising what she wanted him to promise. She wanted to give herself up to the ecstasy he promised, throw caution to the winds, but she'd guarded her heart for so long. This latest episode with Kyla hadn't given her any confidence in the safety of loving.

"Sam, I—"

"Do you love me?" he asked, interrupting her.

She couldn't lie to him. "Yes, but—"

"No. I don't want to hear the *buts*. You said in your note that Kyla and I were the two people you cared about most in the world. You said you trust me with the daughter you love more than life itself.''

"Of course I do. You have no idea how hard it was to write that note and walk away. I just don't want to be like my mother. I don't want to hurt the people I love, and I don't want to be hurt by them.''

"If you trust me with your daughter, can't you trust me with your heart? Can't you trust me to do everything possible to make you happy and not to hurt you? I can't promise that loving me will never cause you any pain, but I can promise to be there and hold you until the pain goes away. I can promise I'll always love you.''

The sun crested the horizon over Sam's shoulder, as if confirming his promises.

Marcie took a deep breath and plunged in. "I love you so much, Sam. So much it's scary.''

"You don't need to be scared. When somebody really loves you, they don't abuse the power that love gives them. Marry me, Marcie. Let's raise our daughter together.''

Marcie couldn't see any reason to hold on to even a remnant of her safe corner any longer. She threw her arms around him and felt his encircle her.

As Sam held her close in the first fragile moments of morning, outside the hospital where their daughter lay recovering, Marcie gave herself to the truly safe feeling of being loved.

Epilogue

Marcie sat in one of the hospital chairs beside Kyla's bed holding Sam's hand.

Sam loved her, she loved him, and Kyla was going to recover from the accident.

But Marcie still wasn't sure her daughter would recover from the emotional shock she'd received the evening before. Would Kyla ever be able to forgive her and accept her as her mother, or would she be *that woman,* just as Rachel's stepmother was?

Kyla opened her eyes and blinked a couple of times. Sam stood, pulling Marcie up with him, but she held back, staying a step behind.

"Hi, Daddy," Kyla said, her voice weak.

"Hi, Princess. How do you feel?"

"Thirsty."

Sam poured water from a pitcher into a plastic glass, adjusted the flexible straw and held it to Kyla's lips.

She sipped briefly. "Thank you, Daddy." She squinted, peering around him. "Is that—?"

"It's me," Marcie said, interrupting and stepping forward before Kyla could call her *that woman*. "I'm so glad you're all right."

Kyla looked back to Sam, and a sharp pain shot through Marcie's heart. She held her breath as she waited to see what Kyla would say.

"I dreamed about my mom." She looked back to Marcie. "My first mom, I mean. There was this long tunnel, and a bright light, and my mom was there. She hugged me and told me how much she missed me."

Marcie wanted to sink through the floor. Kyla's dream had reinforced her memories of Lisa, driving a further wedge between them.

"Then she showed me another baby, a baby named Jenny—"

"*Jenny?*" Marcie repeated, her mouth going dry. She looked at Sam.

He shook his head. "I never told her."

"Yeah, Jenny," Kyla said. "Jennifer Nicole."

"Did my mother tell you about Jenny?" Marcie asked.

"*My* mother told me," she said, sounding a little exasperated by Marcie's obtuseness. "She told me twice so I'd be sure and remember. She said to tell you Jenny is with her and everything's fine."

Marcie clapped a hand to her mouth, and Sam slipped his arm around her waist reassuringly.

Kyla's eyes drifted closed again. "I'm tired," she said.

"Go to sleep," Sam told her. "We'll be here when you wake up."

She opened her eyes again and looked at Marcie. "I almost forgot. She said it was okay for me to call you Mother. If you want me to."

Marcie leaned forward and brushed the blond hair back from Kyla's soft cheek, being careful not to frighten her child with the depth of her emotion. "Yes, I'd like very much for you to call me Mother. But only if you want to."

"Yeah, I kind of like the idea of your being my second mother. But, since I'm thirteen now, I think Mom sounds better."

"I think it sounds wonderful."

Kyla smiled and, apparently satisfied that she'd delivered her message, closed her eyes and returned to a peaceful slumber.

Marcie tucked the cover under her daughter's chin and turned to Sam. "She wants to call me Mom."

He smiled and pulled her into his arms, cupping her cheek and chin in one big hand. "I want to call you Mrs. Woodward. What do you think about that?"

She toyed with a button on his shirt. "That'll be all right for now, but after we've been married for ten years or so, maybe you'll know me well enough to call me Marcie." She looked up at him and gave a light, happy giggle.

His smile widened. "I didn't know you could do that. Giggle, I mean."

"I didn't know it, either. But then, I didn't know I could ever find somebody like you to love."

He pulled her closer. "Me either," he said, his breath warm on her cheek. "A few months ago, I'd never have believed I could love someone as much as I love you. It's amazing, the way we've all been given a second chance for happiness...you, me and Kyla."

"Do you think it's possible that Lisa really..."

He pulled back just far enough to look into her eyes. "Yeah," he said, "I think it's possible. After what I've seen these last few weeks, I can't imagine that anything's *impossible* when it comes to love."

* * * * *

Silhouette Romance is proud to present
Virgin Brides, a brand-new monthly
promotional series by some of the bestselling
and most beloved authors in the romance genre.

In March '98, look for the very first
Virgin Brides novel,

THE PRINCESS BRIDE by Diana Palmer.

Just turn the page for an exciting preview of
Diana Palmer's thrilling new tale...

Chapter One

Tiffany saw him in the distance, riding the big black stallion. It was spring, and that meant roundup. It was not unusual to see the owner of the Lariat ranch in the saddle at dawn lending a hand to rope a stray calf or help work the branding. Kingman Marshall kept fit with ranch work, and despite the fact that he shared an office and a business partnership with Tiffany's father in land and cattle, his staff didn't see a lot of him.

This year, they were using helicopters to mass the far-flung cattle, and they had a corral set up on a wide, flat stretch of land where they could dip the cattle, check them, cut out the calves for branding and separate them from their mothers. It was physically demanding work, and no job for a tenderfoot. King wouldn't let Tiffany near it, but it wasn't a front row seat at the corral that she wanted. If she could just get his attention away from the milling cattle on the wide, rolling plain that led to the Guadalupe River, if he'd just look her way...

Tiffany stood up on a rickety lower rung of the gray

wood fence, avoiding the sticky barbed wire, and waved
her Stetson at him. She was a picture of young elegance in
her tan jodhpurs and sexy pink silk blouse and high black
boots. She was a debutante. Her father, Harrison Blair, was
King's business partner and friend, and if she chased King,
her father encouraged her. It would be a marriage made in
heaven. That is, if she could find some way to convince
King of it. He was elusive and quite abrasively masculine.
It might take more than a young lady of almost twenty-one
with a sheltered, monied background to land him. But, then,
Tiffany had confidence in herself; she was beautiful and
intelligent.

Her long black hair hung to her waist in back, and she
refused to have it cut. It suited her tall, slender figure and
made an elegant frame for her soft, oval face and wide
green eyes and creamy complexion. She had a sunny smile,
and it never faded. Tiffany was always full of fire, burning
with a love of life that her father often said had been reflected in her long-dead mother.

"King!" she called, her voice clear, and it carried in the
early-morning air.

He looked toward her. Even at that distance, she could
see that cold expression in his pale blue eyes, on his lean,
hard face with its finely chiseled features. He was a rich
man. He worked hard, and he played hard. He had women,
Tiffany knew so, but he was nothing if not discreet. He was
a man's man, and he lived like one. There was no playful
boy in that tall, fit body. He'd grown up years ago, the
boyishness driven out of him by a rich, alcoholic father
who demanded blind obedience from the only child of his
shallow, runaway wife.

She watched him ride toward her, easy elegance in the
saddle. He reined in at the fence, smiling down at her with
faint arrogance.

"You're out early, tidbit," he remarked in a deep, velvety voice with just a hint of Texas drawl.

"I'm going to be twenty-one tomorrow," she said pertly. "I'm having a big bash to celebrate, and you have to come. Black tie, and don't you dare bring anyone. You're mine, for the whole evening. It's my birthday and on my birthday I want presents—and you're it. My big present."

His dark eyebrows lifted with amused indulgence. "You might have told me sooner that I was going to be a birthday present," he said. "I have to be in Omaha early Saturday."

"You have your own plane," she reminded him. "You can fly."

"I have to sleep sometimes," he murmured.

"I wouldn't touch that line with a ten-foot pole," she drawled, peeking at him behind her long lashes. "Will you come?"

He lit a cigarette, took a long draw and blew it out with slight impatience. "Little girls and their little whims," he mused. "All right, I'll whirl you around the floor and toast your coming-of-age, but I won't stay. I can't spare the time."

"You'll work yourself to death," she complained, and then became solemn. "You're only thirty-four and you look forty."

"Times are hard, honey," he mused, smiling at the intensity in that glowering young face. "We've had low prices and drought. It's all I can do to keep my financial head above water."

"You could take the occasional break," she advised. "And I don't mean a night on the town. You could get away from it all and just rest."

"They're full up at the Home," he murmured, grinning at her exasperated look. "Honey, I can't afford vacations, not with times so hard. What are you wearing for this coming-of-age party?'' he asked to divert her.

''A dream of a dress. White silk, very low in front, with diamanté straps and a white gardenia in my hair.'' She laughed.

He pursed his lips. He might as well humor her. ''That sounds dangerous,'' he said softly.

''It will be,'' she promised, teasing him with her eyes. ''You might even notice that I've grown up.''

He frowned a little. That flirting wasn't new, but it was disturbing lately. He found himself avoiding little Miss Blair, without really understanding why. His body stirred even as he looked at her, and he moved restlessly in the saddle. She was years too young for him, and a virgin to boot, according to her doting, sheltering father. All those years of obsessive parental protection had led to a very immature and unavailable girl. It wouldn't do to let her too close. Not that anyone ever got close to Kingman Marshall, not even his infrequent lovers. He had good reason to keep women at a distance. His upbringing had taught him too well that women were untrustworthy and treacherous.

''What time?'' he asked on a resigned note.

''About seven?''

He paused thoughtfully for a minute. ''Okay.'' He tilted his wide-brimmed hat over his eyes. ''But only for an hour or so.''

''Great!''

He didn't say goodbye. Of course, he never did. He wheeled the stallion and rode off, man and horse so damn arrogant that she felt like flinging something at his tall head. He was delicious, she thought, and her body felt hot all over just looking at him. On the ground he towered over her, lean and hard-muscled and sexy as all hell. She loved watching him.

With a long, unsteady sigh, she finally turned away and remounted her mare. She wondered sometimes why she bothered hero-worshiping such a man. One of these days he'd get married and she'd just die. God forbid that he'd marry anybody but her!

That was when the first shock of reality hit her squarely between the eyes. Why, she had to ask herself, would a man like that, a mature man with all the worldly advantages, want a young and inexperienced woman like herself at his side? The question worried her so badly that she almost lost control of her mount.

The truth of her situation was unpalatable and a little frightening. She'd never even considered a life without King. What if she had to?

She rode home slowly, a little depressed because she'd had to work so hard just to get King to agree to come to her party. And still haunting her was that unpleasant speculation about a future without King...

But she perked up when she thought of the evening ahead. King didn't come to the house often, only when her father wanted to talk business away from work, or occasionally for drinks with some of her father's acquaintances. To have him come to a party was new and stimulating. Especially if it ended the way she planned. She had her sights well and truly set on the big rancher. Now all she had to do was take aim!

*   *   *   *   *

SANDRA STEFFEN

Continues the twelve-book series— 36 Hours—in February 1998 with Book Eight

MARRIAGE BY CONTRACT

Nurse Bethany Kent could think of only one man who could make her dream come true: Dr. Tony Petrocelli, the man who had helped her save the life of the infant she desperately wanted to adopt. As husband and wife, they could provide the abandoned baby with a loving home. But could they provide each other with more than just a convenient marriage?

For Tony and Bethany and *all* the residents of Grand Springs, Colorado, the storm-induced blackout was just the beginning of 36 Hours that changed *everything!* You won't want to miss a single book.

Available at your favorite retail outlet.

Look us up on-line at: http://www.romance.net

SC36HRS8

Take 4 bestselling love stories FREE

a FREE surprise gift!

Special Limited-time Offer

Mail to Silhouette Reader Service™

3010 Walden Avenue
P.O. Box 1867
Buffalo, N.Y. 14240-1867

YES! Please send me 4 free Silhouette Romance™ novels and my free surprise gift. Then send me 6 brand-new novels every month, which I will receive months before they appear in bookstores. Bill me at the low price of $2.90 each plus 25¢ delivery and applicable sales tax, if any.* That's the complete price and a savings of over 10% off the cover prices—quite a bargain! I understand that accepting the books and gift places me under no obligation ever to buy any books. I can always return a shipment and cancel at any time. Even if I never buy another book from Silhouette, the 4 free books and the surprise gift are mine to keep forever.

215 SEN CF2P

Name	(PLEASE PRINT)	
Address		Apt. No.
City	State	Zip

This offer is limited to one order per household and not valid to present Silhouette Romance™ subscribers. *Terms and prices are subject to change without notice. Sales tax applicable in N.Y.

USROM-696   ©1990 Harlequin Enterprises Limited

Return to the Towers!

In March
New York Times bestselling author

NORA ROBERTS

brings us to the Calhouns' fabulous
Maine coast mansion and reveals the
tragic secrets hidden there for generations.

For all his degrees, Professor Max Quartermain has a
lot to learn about love—and luscious Lilah Calhoun is
just the woman to teach him. Ex-cop Holt Bradford is
as prickly as a thornbush—until Suzanna Calhoun's
special touch makes love blossom in his heart.
And all of them are caught in the race to solve
the generations-old mystery of a priceless
lost necklace…and a timeless love.

Lilah and Suzanna
THE
Calhoun Women

A special 2-in-1 edition containing
FOR THE LOVE OF LILAH and
SUZANNA'S SURRENDER

Available at your favorite retail outlet.